Joseph Forster

Four Great Teachers

John Ruskin, Thomas Carlyle, Ralph Waldo Emerson, and Robert Browning

Joseph Forster

Four Great Teachers
John Ruskin, Thomas Carlyle, Ralph Waldo Emerson, and Robert Browning

ISBN/EAN: 9783337057527

Printed in Europe, USA, Canada, Australia, Japan

Cover: Foto ©Raphael Reischuk / pixelio.de

More available books at **www.hansebooks.com**

FOUR GREAT TEACHERS:

JOHN RUSKIN, THOMAS CARLYLE, RALPH WALDO EMERSON, AND ROBERT BROWNING.

BY

JOSEPH FORSTER.

" Ever their phantoms rise before us,
Our nobler brothers, but one in blood:
At bed and table they lord it o'er us,
With looks of beauty and words of good."

GEORGE ALLEN,

SUNNYSIDE, ORPINGTON,

AND

8, BELL YARD, TEMPLE BAR, LONDON.

1890.

Printed by Hazell, Watson, & Viney, Ld., London and Aylesbury.

NOTE BY THE PUBLISHER.

Only one of these Lectures has appeared before in print, and this has been considerably added to.

CONTENTS.

FOUR GREAT TEACHERS.

I.

JOHN RUSKIN.

PART I.

JOHN RUSKIN is the son of a London merchant, and was born in the year 1819. He thus writes of himself : " Who am I, that I should challenge you," the squires of England, " do you ask ? My mother was a sailor's daughter, and, please you, one of my aunts was a baker's wife, the other a tanner's ; and I don't know much more about my family, except that there used to be a green-grocer of the name in a small shop near the Crystal Palace. Something of my early and vulgar life, if it interests you, I will tell in next 'Fors' ; in this one it is indeed my business, poor gipsy herald as I am, to bring you such a challenge, though you should hunt and hang me for it."

Mr. Ruskin's father came over the Border in search of fortune. " He came up to London, was a clerk in a merchant's office for nine years without a holiday, then began business on his own account, paid his father's debts, and married his exemplary Croydon cousin."

* * * * * *

" My father began business as a wine merchant, with no capital, and a considerable amount of debts bequeathed him by my grandfather.   He accepted the bequest, and paid them all before he began to lay by anything for himself, for which his best friends called him a fool ; and I, without expressing any opinion as to his wisdom, which I knew in such matters to be at least equal to mine, have written on the granite slab over his grave that he was 'an entirely honest merchant.'   As days went on he was able to take a house in Hunter Street, Brunswick Square, No. 54 (the windows of it, fortunately for me, commanded a view of a marvellous iron post, out of which the water-carts were filled through beautiful little trap-doors, by pipes like boa-constrictors, and I was never weary of contemplating that mystery, and the delicious dripping consequent) ; and as years went on he could command a post-chaise and pair for two months in the summer, by help of which, with my mother and me, he went the round of his country customers (who liked to see the principal of the house his own traveller) ; so that at a jog-trot pace, and through the panoramic opening of the four

windows of a post-chaise, made more panoramic
still to me because my seat was a little bracket
in front, I saw all the high-roads and most of
the cross ones of England and Wales, and a great
part of lowland Scotland, as far as Perth, where
every other year we spent the whole summer."

This is how the boy learnt to love art, which,
as he so finely said, "is a translation of nature."
" It happened also—which was the real cause of
the bias of my after life—that my father had a rare
love of pictures. I use the word advisedly, having
never met with another instance of so innate a
faculty for the discernment of true art up to the
point possible without actual practice. Accord-
ingly, wherever there was a gallery to be seen
we stopped at the nearest town for the night ;
and in reverentest manner I thus saw nearly all
the noblemen's houses in England, not, indeed,
myself at that age caring for pictures, but much
for castles and ruins, feeling more and more, as I
grew older, the healthy delight of uncovetous
admiration, and perceiving, as soon as I could
perceive any political truth at all, that it was
probably much happier to live in a small house
and have Warwick Castle to be astonished at,
than to live in Warwick Castle and have nothing
to be astonished at ; but that, at all events, it
would not make Brunswick Square in the least
more pleasantly habitable to pull Warwick Castle
down. And to this day, though I have kind

invitations enough to visit America, I could not, even for a couple of months, live in a country so miserable as to possess no castles."

MR. RUSKIN'S EARLY READING.

" I had Walter Scott's novels and the 'Iliad,' Pope's translation, for my only reading when I was a child on week-days: on Sundays their effect was tempered by ' Robinson Crusoe' and the ' Pilgrim's Progress '; my mother having it deeply in her heart to make an Evangelical clergyman of me. Fortunately, I had an aunt more Evangelical than my mother : and my aunt gave me cold mutton for my Sunday's dinner, which—as I much preferred it hot—greatly diminished the influence of the 'Pilgrim's Progress,' and the end of the matter was that I got all the noble imaginative teaching of Defoe and Bunyan, and yet—am not an Evangelical clergyman. I had, however, still better teaching than theirs, and that compulsorily, and every day of the week. Walter Scott and Pope's Homer were reading of my own election, but my mother forced me, by steady daily toil, to learn long chapters of the Bible by heart, as well as to read it every syllable through, aloud, hard names and all, from Genesis to the Apocalypse, about once a year ; and to that discipline—patient, accurate, and resolute—I owe, not only a knowledge of the book, which I find occasionally serviceable, but much of my general power of taking pains, and the best part of my taste in literature."

The above deeply interesting passage, from "Fors I.," only refers incidentally to Walter Scott; but the following letter contains Mr. Ruskin's matured and fixed opinion on the genius and character of Scott's novels.

"Coniston, *Whit Tuesday*, 1887.

" My dear Sir,—

"You hear a great deal of the worst nonsense ever uttered since men were born on earth. Best hundred books ! Have you ever yet read one good book well ? For a Scotsman, next to his Bible, there is but one book—his native land; but one language—his native tongue ; the sweetest, richest, subtlest, most musical of all the living dialects of Europe. Study your Burns, Scott, and Carlyle. Scott, in his Scottish novels only, and of those only the cheerful ones; with the 'Heart of Midlothian,' but not the 'Bride of Lammermoor,' nor the 'Legend of Montrose,' nor the 'Pirate.' Here is a right list : 'Waverley,' 'Guy Mannering,' 'The Antiquary,' 'Rob Roy,' 'Old Mortality,' 'The Monastery,' 'The Abbot,' 'Redgauntlet,' 'Heart of Midlothian.' Get any of them you can in the old large-print edition when you have a chance, and study every sentence in them. They are models of every virtue in their order of literature, and exhaustive codes of Christian wisdom and ethics. I have written this note with care. I·should be glad that you sent a copy of it to any paper read generally by the students of the University of Edinburgh, and remain, always faithfully yours,

"JOHN RUSKIN."

I cannot comprehend the ground of Mr. Ruskin's exclusion of, perhaps, the greatest and most thrilling romance in any language, "The Bride of Lammermoor," which has been the theme and inspiration of painter and musician. With that exception, I most heartily agree with Mr. Ruskin's noble tribute to the elevated morality and splendid power of the greatest story-teller that ever lived.

In the articles entitled "Fiction: Fair and Foul," which appeared first in the *Nineteenth Century* magazine, and have since been published, with other matter, in three volumes, entitled "On the Old Road," Mr. Ruskin carefully and lovingly analyses some of Scott's novels, and does the fullest justice to the manly dignity, the robust morality, the exquisite purity, the delicate refinement, and the almost Shakespearian humour which flood and float every work of the Great Wizard of the North.

From Hunter Street Mr. Ruskin's father removed to Herne Hill, and from there to a larger house at Denmark Hill.

Before I deal with the great and original teachings of John Ruskin, I think I ought to give a slight sketch of his life. He was born in London in 1819, and educated at Christ Church, Oxford, where he gained the Newdigate prize for poetry ("Salsette and Elephanta") in 1839. When a youth he studied under Copley Fielding and Harding, and soon became enamoured of Turner's glorious works, then but little appreciated.

Turner's splendid "Antwerp" was first sold for £300. It sold not long ago at 6,500 guineas. Ruskin's advocacy of the claims of Turner to the admiration of the world began by a letter he wrote in his defence to *Blackwood's Magazine.* This developed into the first volume of "Modern Painters," which was a great success, and was also bitterly attacked. He resided some time in Italy, and published the remaining volumes of "Modern Painters" between 1846 and 1860. He had previously written the "Seven Lamps of Architecture" (1849) and the "Stones of Venice" (1851 and 1853). He was appointed Rede Lecturer at Cambridge (1867), and Slade Professor of Fine Art at Oxford (1872), but he retired from this position in 1878 in consequence of illness. He again accepted the chair in 1883, and finally vacated it in 1885, owing to the action of the University on the question of vivisection. Besides publishing a great many miscellaneous works—

including " Notes on the Construction of Sheep-
folds," which a simple-minded farmer bought for
practical instruction on the subject, and was very
disappointed and bewildered by its contents—he
gave to the world " Political Economy in Art,"
" Two Paths," " Unto this Last," " Sesame and
Lilies," " Ethics of the Dust," " Queen of the
Air," " Crown of Wild Olive," and " Ariadne
Florentina." In 1871 he commenced his priceless
series of letters entitled " Fors Clavigera," which
he explained meant " Deed, Patience, and Love."

These beautiful letters deal in a strikingly
original and exquisitely beautiful way with nearly
every subject interesting to people of thought,
culture, and refinement. This publication, consisting of ninety-six numbers, was finally closed
in December 1884. Mr. Ruskin is now engaged
on his Autobiography, to the completion of which
the civilised world looks forward with eager
interest.

I will now endeavour to deal with some of the
salient characteristics of Mr. Ruskin's teaching.
To understand Ruskin it is, I think, necessary to
understand Wordsworth. The same loving study
and reverent worship of nature animated both
writers. Ruskin is simply saturated with Wordsworth. The difference between them is one of
temper. One was calm, philosophical, withdrawn
from the cantankerous controversies of politics
and the little details of daily life. John Ruskin,

with a chivalrous disregard of the wear-and-tear
consequent upon mingling in the dusty daily fray,
breaks out here with a letter, and there with a
lecture, dealing directly with the topic of the hour.
He is constantly tapped by the foolishest people.
There is, I must admit, a decided note of feminity
in his genius ; a want of manly strength and
repose—a quality in which Wordsworth was
nearly as great as Goethe.   The voice is piercing
sweet, but it is a falsetto now and then; a head
and not a chest voice; and reminds me occasionally of the unnatural *soprani* of Handel's time.
Mr. Ruskin appears to me now and then to lose
his balance, his common sense.   I do not consider
that he is always a safe teacher to ordinary men
and women ; but to those who can weigh, measure,
and discriminate between his opinions, and as a
noble and chivalrous denouncer of the infinite
vulgarity and stupid greed of the age, his
teachings are of unspeakable value.

The following passage from Wordsworth's
" Excursion " will, I hope, support my opinion
of the similarity of Ruskin's teaching to that of
Wordsworth :—

" How beautiful this dome of sky !
    And the vast hills, in fluctuation fixed
    At thy command, how awful !   Shall the Soul,
    Human and rational, report of thee
    Even less than these ?—Be mute who will, who can
    Yet I will praise thee with impassioned voice :

My lips, that may forget thee in the crowd,
Cannot forget thee here ; where thou hast built
For thy own glory, in the wilderness !
Me didst thou constitute a priest of thine,
In such a temple as we now behold
Reared for thy presence : therefore, am I bound
To worship, here, and everywhere—as one
Not doomed to ignorance, though forced to tread,
From childhood up, the ways of poverty ;
From unreflecting ignorance preserved,
And from debasement rescued.—By thy grace
The particle divine remained unquenched ;
And, 'mid the wild weeds of a rugged soil,
Thy bounty caused to flourish deathless flowers,
From paradise transplanted : wintry age
Impends ; the frost will gather round my heart ;
If the flowers wither, I am worse than dead !—
Come, labour, when the worn-out frame requires
Perpetual Sabbath ; come, disease and want,
And sad exclusion through decay of sense ;
But leave me unabated trust in thee,
And let thy favour, to the end of life,
Inspire me with ability to seek
Repose and hope among eternal things—
Father of heaven and earth ! and I am rich,
And will possess my portion in content !"

The sublime spirit pervading the above lines,
worthy of Milton himself, shines through all
John Ruskin's best work.

A little further on the same great poet,
scorning self, sings :—

" But, above all, the victory is most sure
For him who, seeking faith by virtue, strives
To yield entire submission to the law
Of conscience—conscience reverenced and obeyed,

As God's most intimate presence in the soul,
And his most perfect image in the world.
Endeavour thus to live ; these rules regard ;
These helps solicit ; and a steadfast seat
Shall then be yours among the happy few
Who dwell on earth, yet breathe empyreal air—
Sons of the morning.''

John Ruskin has breathed " empyreal air."
He is, if ever man was, a " son of the morning."

A great deal has been said and written about
Pre-Raphaelitism, with its manly scorn of conventional cant and shallow pretence in art.
Millais, Rossetti, Holman Hunt, and Burne Jones
put their original and daring ideas in glowing
colours before the jaded public, and John Ruskin,
in words not less glowing and opalescent, fought
their battle as he only can fight.

This band of earnest and devoted men of genius
led a revolt against the tea-trays gone wrong of
the Royal Academy. They believed that " the
open secret of nature " must be studied on the
spot ; that an artist was not a man who slavishly
imitated the method of some successful painter ;
but one who with devoted love pursued the glow,
the glitter, or the sad solemnity of nature with a
never-failing energy and perseverance. According
to a man's insight into nature and his power to
make us feel by his picture what he felt when
he looked at and loved the scene portrayed, is
the value of his genius. That is not done by
making a worse copy of a bad picture ; or painting

—as Doré used to paint—from drawings and a fertile imagination.

Reynolds told his pupils to generalise, and not to degrade art by details. But, thank heaven! his practice contradicted his teachings, and in spite of a vicious theory, his pictures proved him a great genius, drawing his inspiration from the bottomless well of nature. This is Mr. Ruskin's own definition of Pre-Raphaelitism:—

"Pre-Raphaelitism has but one principle, that of absolute, uncompromising truth in all that it does, obtained by working everything, down to the most minute detail, from nature, and from nature only; or, where imagination is necessarily trusted to, always endeavouring to conceive a fact as it really was likely to have happened. Every Pre-Raphaelite landscape background is painted, to the last touch, in the open air, from the thing itself. Every Pre-Raphaelite figure, however studied in expression, is a true portrait of some living person. Every minute accessory is painted in the same manner. This is the main Pre-Raphaelite principle."

I don't think any one can doubt that the influence of this teaching has been good. It brought the artist back to the direct study of the all-mother, Nature ; and that is always good and wholesome.

"But art is not nature, or it would not be art." And those of us who have seen some of the best pictures of the school, painted with all the glow of youthful enthusiasm, must admit that many of them were hard and unpleasing. Art must please first, I think, and refine and elevate the mind and heart too. A man may think he has a mission to teach ; but he must also prove, if he wishes to be regarded by a busy world, that he can teach in a pleasing, graceful way. Mere scolding at large will not do. That leads me to the exquisite beauty, finish, and grace of John Ruskin's literary style. One would, I think, rather read the melodious scoldings of Ruskin than the praise of most other writers. His very faults are better than their puny literary virtues.

I will now venture to quote a few passages from this great writer and teacher. In speaking of Reynolds, Ruskin writes : " Sir Joshua Reynolds threw himself at the feet of the great masters of Italy, and arose to share their throne. . . . He had a strong, unaided, unerring instinct for all that was true, pure, and noble."

In speaking of Turner's " Slave Ship," he wrote : " Its daring conception, ideal in the highest sense of the word, is based on the purest truth, and wrought out with the concentrated knowledge of a life. The whole picture is dedicated to the most sublime of subjects and impressions—the power, majesty, and deathfulness of the open, deep, illimitable sea."

Again, he writes : " Fine Art is that in which

the hand, the head, and the heart go together.
Greatness of art consists, first, in earnest and
intense seizing of natural facts ; then in ordering
these facts by strength of human intellect, so
as to make them, for all who look upon them, to
the utmost serviceable, memorable, and beautiful.
And thus great art is nothing else than the type
of strong and noble life; for as the ignoble person,
in the dealing with all that occurs in the world
about him, sees nothing clearly—looks nothing
firmly in the face, and then allows himself to be
swept away by the torrent and inexorable force
of the things that he would not foresee and could
not understand,—so the noble person, looking the
facts of the world full in the face, and fathoming
them with deep faculty, then deals with them, in
unalarmed intelligence and unhurried strength,
and becomes, with his human intellect and will,
no unconscious nor insignificant agent in com-
municating their good and restraining their evil.

"Homer sang what he saw ; Phidias carved
what he saw ; Raphael painted the men and
women in their own caps and mantles; and every
man who has arisen to eminence in modern times
has done so by working in their way and doing
the things he saw. Base Academy teaching, in
spite of which these men have risen, I say in
spite of the entire method and aim of our art
teaching : it destroys the greater number ; it
hinders and paralyses the greatest."

MR. RUSKIN ON CLOUDS.

Who can gauge the priceless, the unspeakable value of the following passage, opening as it does a world of exquisite and ever-varying beauty to the eye of every human being willing to raise his or her eyes from the dead pavement to the glorious panorama of the "brave o'erhanging firmament"!

"It is a strange thing how little in general people know about the sky. It is the part of creation in which nature has done more for the sake of pleasing man, more for the sole and evident purpose of talking to him and teaching him, than in any other of her works, and it is just the part in which we least attend to her. There are not many of her other works in which some more material or essential purpose than the mere pleasing of man is not answered by every part of their organization ; but every essential purpose of the sky might, so far as we know, be answered, if once in three days, or thereabouts, a great, ugly, black rain-cloud were brought up over the blue, and everything well watered, and so all left blue again till next time, with perhaps a film of morning and evening mist for dew. And instead of this, there is not a moment in any day of our lives, when nature is not producing scene after scene, picture after picture, glory after glory,

and working still upon such exquisite and constant
principles of the most perfect beauty, that it is
quite certain it is all done for us, and intended
for our perpetual pleasure. And every man,
wherever placed, however far from other sources
of interest or of beauty, has this doing for
him constantly. The noblest scenes of the earth
can be seen and known but by few ; it is not
intended that man should live always in the
midst of them ; he injures them by his presence,
he ceases to feel them if he be always with them :
but the sky is for all ; bright as it is, it is not

> ' Too bright or good
> For human nature's daily food ';

it is fitted in all its functions for the perpetual
comfort and exalting of the heart, for the soothing
it and purifying it from its dross and dust. Sometimes gentle, sometimes capricious, sometimes
awful, *never* the same for two moments together ;
almost human in its passions, almost spiritual in its
tenderness, almost Divine in its infinity, its appeal
to whatever is immortal in us is as distinct, as its
ministry of chastisement or of blessing to what
is mortal is essential. And yet we never attend
to it, we never make it a subject of thought, but
as it has to do with our animal sensations : we
look upon all by which it speaks to us more
clearly than to brutes, upon all which bears
witness to the intention of the Supreme that we

are to receive more from the covering vault than
the light and the dew which we share with the weed
and the worm, only as a succession of meaning-
less and monotonous accident, too common and
too vain to be worthy of a moment of watchful-
ness or a glance of admiration. If in our moments
of utter idleness or insipidity, we turn to the sky
as a last resource, which of its phenomena do we
speak of ? One says it has been wet ; and another,
it has been windy ; and another, it has been warm.
Who, among the whole chattering crowd, can tell
me of the forms and the precipices of the chain of
tall white mountains that girded the horizon at
noon yesterday ? Who saw the narrow sunbeam
that came out of the south and smote upon their
summits until they melted and mouldered away
in a dust of blue rain ? Who saw the dance of
the dead clouds when the sunlight left them last
night, and the west wind blew them before it like
withered leaves ? All has passed unregretted as
unseen ; or if the apathy be ever shaken off, even
for an instant, it is only by what is gross, or
what is extraordinary ; and yet it is not in the
broad and fierce manifestations of the elemental
energies, *not* in the clash of the hail, nor the drift
of the whirlwind, that the highest characters of
the sublime are developed. God is not in the
earthquake, nor in the fire, *but in the still, small
voice.* They are but the blunt and the low faculties
of our nature, which can only be addressed through

2

lampblack and lightning.   It is in quiet and
subdued passages of unobtrusive majesty, the
deep, and the calm, and the perpetual ; that which
must be sought ere it is seen, and loved ere it is
understood ; things which the angels work out
for us daily and yet very eternally : which are
never wanting, and never repeated ; which are to
be found always, yet each found but once ; it is
through these that the lesson of devotion is chiefly
taught, and the blessing of beauty given.   These
are what the artist of highest aim must study ;
it is these, by the combination of which his ideal
is to be created ; these, of which so little notice
is ordinarily taken by common observers, that
I fully believe, little as people in general are
concerned with art, more of their ideas of sky
are derived from pictures than from reality ; and
that if we could examine the conception formed
in the minds of most educated persons when we
talk of clouds, it would frequently be found composed of fragments of blue and white reminiscences
of the old masters."—" *Modern Painters*," vol. i.,
sec. iii., cap. i.

Part II.

" Man's use and function are to be the witness
of the glory of God, and to advance that glory
by his reasonable obedience and resultant happiness.   Better not to live, than that we should
disappoint the purpose of existence."

The following passage is very characteristic of Mr. Ruskin : " Many people appear to believe that homes and lands, and food and raiment were alone useful, and as if sight, thought, and admiration were all profitless. Men who think, as far as such men can think, that the meat is more than the life, and the raiment than the body, who look to the world as a stable, and to its fruit as fodder ; vine dressers and husbandmen, who love the corn they grind, and the grapes they crush, better than the gardens of the angels upon the slopes of Eden ; hewers of wood and drawers of water, who think that it is to give them wood to hew and water to draw that the pine forests cover the mountains like the shadow of God, and the great rivers move like His Eternity. . . . The Nebuchadnezzar curse, that sends men to grass like oxen, seems to follow too closely on the excess or continuance of national power and peace."

* * * * * *

" When the honour of God is thought to consist in the poverty of His temple—when we ravage without a pause of remorse all the loveliness of creation which God in giving pronounced Good—there is need, bitter need, to bring back to men's minds, that to live is nothing, unless to live be to know Him by whom we live, and that He is not to be known by marring His fair works, and blotting out the evidence of His influences

upon His creations ; not amidst the hurry of
crowds and crash of innovation, but in solitary
places, and out of the glowing intelligences which
He gave to men of old."

And, may I add, to such men as John Ruskin,
Thomas Carlyle, Emerson, and Browning of our
own day ?

*   *   *   *   *   *

" The true sign of good breeding is sympathy :
a vulgar man is kind in a hard way on principle ;
whereas a highly bred man, even when cruel,
will be cruel in a softer way, understanding and
feeling what he inflicts, and pitying his victim."

*   *   *   *   *   *

" Impossible to be open, except to men of his
own kind. To them he can open himself, by a
word or glance ; but to men not of his own kind
he cannot open himself though he tried it through
an eternity of clear grammatical speech. By the
very acuteness of his sympathy he knows how
much he can give to anybody, and he gives that
frankly."

*   *   *   *   *   *

" We have among mankind in general the three
orders of beings : the lowest, sordid and selfish,
which neither sees nor feels ; the second, noble
and sympathetic, but which sees and feels without concluding or acting ; the third and highest,
which loses sight in resolution, and feeling in
work. For one who is blinded to the works of

God by profound abstraction or lofty purpose, tens of thousands have their eyes sealed by vulgar selfishness, and their intelligence crushed by impious care."

The following passage is exquisitely beautiful and true : " A man of genius remains in great part a child, seeing with the large eyes of children, in perpetual wonder, not conscious of much knowledge—conscious, rather, of infinite ignorance, and yet infinite power ; a fountain of eternal admiration, delight, and creative force within him meeting the ocean of visible and governable things around him."

What a thrill of love pervades and pulses through this : " All things are literally better, lovelier, and more beloved for the imperfections which have been divinely appointed, that the law of human life may be Effort, and the law of human judgment—Mercy."

How closely that passage applies to the criticism I have ventured to make on Mr. Ruskin (page 9) ! His very faults truly increase our love for him.

* * * * * *

" Justice, mercy, and truth, and no mention of any doctrinal point whatsoever occurring in either piece of Divine teaching, viz., Book of Job and the Sermon on the Mount."

* * * * * *

The following powerful passage is well worthy of deep consideration in this noisy day of rant and cant : " It is not accident, it is not Heaven-commanded calamity, it is not the original and inevitable evil of man's nature, which fill your streets with lamentation, and your graves with prey. It is only that, when there should have been labour, there has been lasciviousness ; and wilfulness, when there should have been sub-ordination."

To return to art, Mr. Ruskin in a magnificent passage, writes, " The gifts which distinctly mark the artist—without which he must be feeble in life, forgotten in death, with which he may become one of the shakers of the earth and one of the signal lights of heaven—are those of sympathy and imagination.

" Greatness is not a teachable nor gainable thing, but the expression of the mind of a God-made great man : teach, or preach, or labour as you will, everlasting difference is set between one man's capacity and another's ; and the God-given supremacy is the priceless thing, always just as rare in the world at one time as another.

" I believe that the first test of a truly great man is his humility. I do not mean by humility, doubt of his power, or hesitation in speaking his opinions ; but a right understanding of the rela-tion between what he can do or say, and the rest of the world's sayings and doings. All great men not only know their own business, but usually that they know it, and are not only right in their main opinions, but usually know that they are right in them; only they do not think much of themselves on that account. Arnolfo knows that he can build a good dome at Florence.

" Albert Durer writes calmly to one who had found fault with his work, ' It cannot be better done'; Sir Isaac Newton knows that he has worked out a problem or two that would have puzzled anybody else; only they do not expect their fellowmen therefore to fall down and worship them; they have a curious undersense of powerlessness, feeling that the greatness is not in them, but through them; they could not do or be anything else than God made them. And they see something Divine and God-made in every other man they meet, and are endlessly, foolishly, incredibly merciful."

Mr. Ruskin, in the following passage, divides men into three ranks and four classes: " Three ranks—1st, the man who perceives rightly because he does not feel; 2nd, the man who perceives wrongly because he feels; and then, lastly, there is the man who perceives rightly in spite of his feeling. There are four classes: the men who feel nothing and therefore see truly; the men who feel strongly, think weakly, and see untruly (2nd order of poets); and the men who feel strongly, think strongly, and see truly (1st order of poets); and the men who, strong as human creatures can be, are yet submitted to influences stronger than they, and see in a sort untruly, because what they see is inconceivably above them. This last is the usual condition of prophetic inspiration."

The following passage on women and their influence occurs in Mr. Ruskin's lecture on Classic and Gothic Art, delivered at Oxford: " Although in an ideal state of society the women will be the guiding and purifying power, in savage and undeveloped countries they are openly oppressed as beasts of burden, in corrupted and fallen countries more secretly and terribly. There is a surplus of women, an apparent glut of them ; but of the useful women, the best kind of women, the supply, small to begin with, is diminished by death and misguidance. The experience of most thoughtful persons will confirm me in saying that extremely good girls usually die young. Little Nells and May Queens fly from the smoke and stir of this dim spot which men call earth to the regions mild of calm and serene air. Most persons of affectionate temper have lost their own May Queens or Little Nells in their time, and I could count the like among my best-loved friends with a rosary of tears. A country paying this enforced tax of its good girls annually to heaven, ought at least to take great care of those it has left. Passing by those who go into convents, or become sick nurses and do much good, there is a kind of girl just as

good, but with a less strong will, who is more
or less spoilable and mismanageable; and these
are almost sure to come to grief by the faults
of others or merely by the general fortunes and
chances of the world." Mr. Ruskin tells, in his
own exquisite way, a pathetic story of a sea
captain's daughter; "the most beautiful girl of
the pure English Greek type, finely pencilled
dark brows, rather dark hair, and bright pure
colour, who, after refusing many lovers, fell in
love with a youth whom, with foolish pride, she
treated worse than all the others, so that he lost
hope, and soon after died. After his death she
realized the depth and value of the love she had
lost, and never recovered from the blow. She
wandered about sadly and listlessly for some
years, and then died of a rapid decline."

Mr. Ruskin's opinions on love are as original
and daring as his views on other subjects. In
his opinion a father is a girl's proper confidant
rather than her mother. "What she is not
inclined to tell her father should be told to no
one, and in nine cases out of ten not thought
of by herself. I believe that few fathers, however wrong-headed or hard-hearted, would fail
of answering the habitual and patient confidence
of their child with true care for her." Then
Mr. Ruskin, in his emphatic manner, lays down
the following ideal law of courtship, which, I venture to believe, is as little likely to be followed

as his suggestion that a girl should confide in her
father in preference to her mother.

" When a youth is fully in love with a girl, and
feels that he is wise in loving her, he should at
once tell her so plainly and take his chance
bravely with other suitors. No lover should
have the insolence to think of being accepted
at once, nor should any girl have the cruelty to
refuse at once without severe reasons. If she
simply doesn't like him, she may send him away
for seven years or so, he vowing to live on cresses
and wear sackcloth meanwhile, or the like
penance ; if she likes him a little, or thinks she
might come to like him in time, she may let him
stay near her, putting him always on sharp trial
to see what stuff he is made of, and requiring
figuratively as many lion-skins or giants' heads
as she thinks herself worth. The whole meaning
and power of true courtship is probation, and it
ought not to be shorter than three years at least ;
seven is, to my mind, the orthodox time. And
these relations between the young people should
be openly and simply known, not to their friends
only, but to everybody who has the least interest
in them ; and a girl worth anything ought always
to have half a dozen or so suitors under love for
her."

This is simply lovely in its pure Arcadian
simplicity. It is like reading the almost Divine
" Faërie Queen " of Spenser. What Mr. Ruskin

asks for belongs to that fairyland, a place somewhere between earth and heaven.

A little farther on **Mr.** Ruskin attacks in his
most trenchant way the vulgar "mob courtship"
of to-day.

"There are no words strong enough to express the general danger and degradation of the
manners of mob courtship, as distinct from these
which have become the fashion, almost the law,
in modern times : when, in a miserable confusion
of candle-light, moonlight, and lime-light—and
anything but daylight—in indecently attractive
and insanely expensive dresses, in snatched
moments, in hidden corners, in accidental im-
pulses and dismal ignorances, young people smirk
and ogle and whisper and whimper and sneak and
stumble and flutter and fumble and blunder into
what they call love, expect to get whatever they
like the moment they fancy it, and are continually
in the danger of losing all the honour of life for
a folly, and all the joy of it by an accident."

Mr. Ruskin speaks with pathetic power of
"lost jewels," girls with "little power of ruling
and every provocation of mis-ruling their fates,
who have from their births much against them,
few to help, and virtually none to guide them.
If there be fire and genius in these neglected
ones, and they chance to have beauty also, God
save them and all of us ! What do these bright
reverses of their best human treasures not cost

the economical British race or the cheerful French
—this casting away of things precious, the pro-
fanation of things pure, the pain of things
capable of happiness,—to what sum incalculable
do these amount to ? "

Mr. Ruskin sadly ponders on these terrible
facts as he looks down on "all the south and
east of Lancashire and Yorkshire, black with the
fume of their fever-fretted cities, rolling itself
along the dales and mixed with the torrent
mists."

Mr. Ruskin's defence from ignorant and pre-
judiced attacks is most valuable and interesting.

" It is quite possible for the simplest workman or labourer for whom I write to understand
what the feelings of a gentleman are, and share
them, if he will ; but the crisis and horror of
this present time are that its desire of money,
and the fulness of luxury dishonestly attainable
by common persons, are gradually making churls
of all men ; and the nobler passions are not
merely disbelieved, but even the conception of
them seems ludicrous to the impotent churl
mind ; so that, to take only so poor an instance
of them as my own life—because I have passed
it in almsgiving, not in fortune-hunting ; because I have laboured always for the honour of
others, not my own, and have chosen rather to
make men look to Turner and Luini, than to
form or exhibit the skill of my own hand ; be-

cause I have lowered my rents, and assured the
comfortable lives of my poor tenants, instead of
taking from them all I could force for the roofs
they needed; because I love a wood walk better
than a London street ; and would rather watch
a seagull fly than shoot it, and rather hear a
thrush sing than eat it ; finally, because I never
disobeyed my mother, because I have honoured
all women with solemn worship, and have been
kind even to the unthankful and the evil ; therefore the hacks of English art and literature wag
their heads at me, and the poor wretch who
pawns the dirty linen of his soul for a bottle of
sour wine and a cigar talks of the effeminate
sentimentality of Ruskin."—" *Fors*," IV.

A few words on the St. George's Society,
formed by Mr. Ruskin with the intention of
grappling with some of the evils which he describes with unequalled eloquence and power.

I will again quote the great teacher on the
aim of the Society :—

" The highest possible education of English
men and women living by agriculture in their
native land, I do not care where the land is nor
of what quality. I would rather it should be
poor, for I want space more than food. I will
make the best of it that I can at once by wage
labour, under the best agricultural advice. I
should like a bit of marsh land of small value,
which I would trench with alternate ridge and

canal, changing it all into solid land, and deep
water to be farmed in fish. If, instead, I got a
rocky piece, I should arrange reservoirs for rain,
then put what earth is sprinkled on it into work-
able masses ; and ascertaining in either case how
many mouths the gained spaces of ground will
easily feed, put upon them families chosen for
me by old landlords who know their people and
can send me cheerful and honest ones, accustomed
to obey orders and live in the fear of God. If
any young couples of the higher classes choose
to accept such rough life, I would rather have
them for tenants than any others. Tenants, I
say, and at long leases if they behave well, with
power eventually to purchase the piece of land
they live on for themselves, if they can save the
price of it; the rent they pay meanwhile being
the tithe of the annual produce to St. George's
Fund. The modes of cultivation of the land to
be under the control of the overseer of the whole
estate, appointed by the trustees of the fund ;
but the tenants shall build their own houses to
their own minds, under certain conditions as to
materials and strength; and have for themselves
the entire produce of the land, except the tithe
aforesaid. The children will be required to
attend training schools for bodily exercise and
music, with such education as I have already
described. Every household will have its library
given it from the fund, and consisting of a fixed

number of volumes, some constant, the others chosen by each family out of a list of permitted books, from which they afterwards may increase the library if they choose. The formation of this library, for choice, by a republication of classical authors in standard forms, has long been a main object with me. No newspapers, nor any books but those named in the annually renewed lists, are to be allowed in any household. In time I hope to get a journal published containing notice of any really important matters taking place in this or other countries, or the closely sifted truth of them."

Part III.

I once heard Mr. Ruskin lecture at the Working Men's College, Great Ormond Street. That must have been twenty-five years ago. Mr. Ruskin's manner as a lecturer was charming— so easy, so unaffected, and yet, every now and then, soaring easily upwards to a noble pitch of earnest eloquence. The lecture was on a British penny, which he compared with a Greek coin, pointing out, with fine wit and satire, the grovelling vulgarity of the one, and the exquisite purity of line and harmony of design in the other. He was very earnest on that occasion, and, I think, on every occasion, in pointing out to his hearers the terrible social dangers by which we are surrounded and may be overwhelmed.

In fact, the lecture was full of deep feeling, the subtlest art criticism, and was illuminated now and again by fine caustic wit and masterly irony.

The following graphic sketch of Mr. Ruskin will, I am sure, be appreciated by my readers :—

" Mr. Ruskin rises early, and writes for three hours before his guests are down. Breakfast over, he retires to his study to answer letters or complete some piece of unfinished work, or will go out on the hill, perhaps, and make a delicately finished study of rock and grass for the engraver's hand to copy.

" Between one and six o'clock, the tourist at the Lakes may see a slight figure dressed in a grey frock-coat, and wearing the bright blue tie so familiar to audiences at Oxford and elsewhere, walking about the quiet lanes, sitting down by the harbour's side, or rowing on the water. The back is somewhat bent, the light brown hair straight and long, the whiskers scarcely show signs of eight-and-fifty summers numbered, and the spectator need not be surprised at the determined energy with which a boat is brought to shore or pushed out into the lake.

" Sometimes a friend breaks on this peaceful time, and is met with both hands outstretched, while the gentle look in the clear blue eyes and a few low-voiced words give him full assurance that he is entirely welcome. To such the place is gladly shown ; and a walk is taken up the grass paths cut through the woods, with seats placed where the views are best, to look out over mountain and lake, and be taught, maybe, in the rich colours and fleecy clouds, the utter rightness of Turner ; till, ascending higher, an admiring eye must be cast on a bit of rough ground, red with heather, which, lying just beyond the boundaries of Brantwood, is the Professor's Naboth's Vineyard.

" Mr. Ruskin's sensitive nature is singularly affected by changes of weather, and a bright day makes him as joyful as a dull one makes him sad. But courtesy and kindness to those around him are characteristics he never loses ; insincerity is a fault of which he is thoroughly devoid ; and those who know him best delight in an unaffected simplicity of manner, which in men of acknow-ledged genius is as valuable as it is often rare."

In this slight sketch of Mr. Ruskin I have, by a careful selection of quotations, endeavoured to bring out clearly the light and shade of his cha-racter and genius. I shall conclude my article by two quotations which, I think, for power, scope, and elevation, are unsurpassed and un-surpassable : they place Ruskin by the side of

Carlyle and Emerson, as one of the greatest and most stimulating teachers of the century.

" Whatever may be the inability in this present life to mingle the full enjoyment of the Divine works with the full discharge of every practical duty—and confessedly in many cases this must be—let us not attribute the inconsistency to any indigency of the faculty of contemplation, but to the sin and suffering of the fallen state, and the change of order from the keeping of the garden to the tilling of the ground. We cannot say how far it is right or agreeable with God's will, while men are perishing round about us, while grief, and pain, and wrath, and impiety, and death, and all the powers of the air are working wildly and evermore, and the cry of blood going up to heaven, that any of us should take hand from the plough ; but this we know, that there will come a time when the service of God shall be the beholding of Him ; and though in these stormy seas, where we are now driven up and down, His Spirit is dimly seen on the face of the waters, and we are left to cast anchors out of the stern and wish for the day—that day will come— when, with the evangelists on the crystal and stable sea, all the creatures of God shall be full of eyes within, and there shall be 'no more curse, but His servants shall serve Him, and shall see His face.'"

The following sublime passage, which, I think,

sums up all the beauty, intellectual and moral, contained in all Mr. Ruskin's works, shall terminate my article :—

" Here is a short piece of precious word revelation, for instance—'God is love.' Love! yes. But what is that? The revelation does not tell you that, I think. Look into the mirror, and you will see. Out of your own heart you may know what love is. In no other possible way, by no other help or sign. All the words and sounds ever uttered, all the revelations of cloud, or flame, or crystal, are utterly powerless. They cannot tell you, in the smallest point, what love means. Only the broken mirror (the soul) can. Here is more revelation. God is just. Just! What is that? The revelation cannot help you to discover. You say it is dealing equitably or equally. But how do you discover the equality? Not by inequality of mind, not by a mind incapable of weighing, judging, or distributing. If the lengths seem unequal in the broken mirror, for you they are unequal; but if they seem equal, then the mirror is true. So far as you recognize equality, and your conscience tells you what is just, so far your mind is the image of God's ; and so far as you do not discern the nature of justice or equality, the words 'God is just' bring no revelation to you.

" But His thoughts are not as our thoughts. No ; the sea is not a standing pool by the wayside.

Yet when the breeze crisps the pool you may see the image of the breakers and a likeness of the foam. Nay, in some sort, the same foam. If the sea is for ever invisible to you, something you may learn from the pool. Nothing assuredly, any otherwise. But this poor miserable Me! Is this, then, all the book I have got to read God in? Yes! truly so. No other book, or fragment of a book, than that will you ever find. No velvet-bound missal, nor frankincensed manuscript; nothing hieroglyphic nor cuneiform; papyrus and pyramid are alike silent on this matter; nothing in the clouds above or the earth beneath. That flesh-bound volume is the only revelation that is, that was, or that can be. In that is the image of God painted; in that is the law of God written; in that is the promise of God revealed. Know thyself, for through thyself only canst thou know God. In the glass darkly. But except through the glass, in no wise.

" A tremendous crystal, waved in water, poured out upon the ground; you may defile it, despise it, pollute it, at your pleasure and at your peril; for on the peace of those weak waves must all the heaven you shall ever gain be first seen; and through such purity as you can ensure for those dark waves must all the light of the risen Sun of righteousness be bent down by faint refraction. Cleanse them and calm them, as you love your life.

"Therefore is it that all the power of nature depends in subjection to the human soul. Man is the sun of the world, more than the real sun. The fire of his wonderful heart is the only light and heat worth gauge and measure.

"Where he is, is the tropics. Where he is not, the ice world."

> "Once read thy own breast right,
>   And thou hast done with fears.
> Man gets no other light,
>   Search he a thousand years."

"Sink in thyself; there ask what ails thee, at that shrine."

NOTE.

The *Birmingham Daily Post*, October 29th, 1887, referring to my paper on "John Ruskin," said, "We note one curious little point. The writer devotes a page or two to Wordsworth, because, as he says, to understand Ruskin it is necessary to understand Wordsworth, adding, 'Ruskin is simply saturated with Wordsworth.' Now, within the few last weeks a little book has appeared with the title, 'Books that have Influenced Me,' and Mr. Ruskin is one of the men of mark who supply auto-biographic information on this point. Mr. Ruskin gives Horace, Pindar, Dante, Scott, Pope, Byron, Coleridge, Keats, Burns, Molière, etc., but he does not, either in his list or in a supplementary letter, so much as allude to Wordsworth."

In the *Century* of January 1888, an interesting, although, in my opinion, very unfair article on John Ruskin appeared, written by Mr. W. J. Stillman, who at one time was on very intimate terms with his subject. Curious to say, the article contained a complete confirmation of my opinion as to Ruskin's loving appreciation of and affinity with Wordsworth, in the form of a letter from the great teacher and art critic to Mr. Stillman, published for the first time in the article referred to, in which, with characteristic zeal, Mr. Ruskin recommends certain books. "You should read much—and generally old books ; but above all avoid German books—and all Germanists except Carlyle, whom read as much as you can or like ; read George Herbert and Spenser, and Wordsworth and Homer, all constantly."

THOMAS CARLYLE.

THOMAS CARLYLE was born on the 4th December, 1795, in the parish of Middlebie, near Ecclefechan, Dumfriesshire. His father was "earnest, energetic, of quick intellect, and in earlier life somewhat passionate and pugnacious. He was not just the man to be popular among his rustic neighbours of Annandale; but they respected his pronounced individuality, felt his strong will, and his terse, epigrammatic sayings were remembered and repeated many years after his death (1833). In the latter years of his life he became a more decidedly religious character, and the natural asperities of his disposition and manner were much softened."

The above vivid portrait of Carlyle's father was drawn by an aged Scotch minister who knew him well, and was quoted by Mr. Moncure D. Conway in his admirable article on Thomas Carlyle in *Harper's Magazine*.

On one occasion the old Spartan father was very ill during harvest time. No work in the fields for him; nothing but water-gruel, doctor's stuff, and special prayers. Not a bit of it ! He crawled to the fields in the early morning. The corn was ripe for the sickle. He stamped on the ground, and said, " *I'll gar mysel' work at t' harvest.*" *And he did it.* A reverend gentleman once favoured the congregation of Mr. Carlyle's church with a graphic description of the horrors of eternal punishment. James Carlyle listened to him till he had finished; but then came out of his pew, and placing himself before the clergyman said, " Ay, ye may thump and stare till yer een start fra their sockets, but ye'll na gar me believe such stuff as that." So much for Carlyle's very vertebrate father. Now a few words on his mother. Here again I quote Carlyle's words to Mr. Conway, the friend and not the Froude of Carlyle.

" My mother stands in my memory as beautiful in all that makes the excellence of woman. Pious and gentle she was, with an unweariable devotedness to her family; a loftiness of moral aim and religious conviction which gave her presence and her humble home a sort of graciousness, and, even as I see it now, dignity; and with it, too, a good deal of wit and originality of mind. No man had better opportunities than I for comprehending, were they comprehensible, the great depths of a mother's love for her children. Nearly my first profound impressions in this world are connected with the death of an infant

sister—an event whose sorrowfulness was made
known to me in the inconsolable grief of my
mother. For a long time she seemed to dissolve
in tears—only tears. For several months not one
night passed but she dreamed of holding her babe
in her arms and clasping it to her breast. At
length, one morning she related a change in her
dream : while she held the child in her arms it
had seemed to break up into small fragments,
and so crumbled away and vanished. From that
night her vision of the babe and dream of clasping
it never returned.

"The only fault I can remember in my mother
was her being too mild and peaceful for the
planet she lived in. [*Let us thank Heaven her
son did not sin in that way!*] When I was sent
to school, she piously enjoined upon me that I
should, under no conceivable circumstances, fight
with any boy, nor resist any evil done to me ;
and her instructions were so solemn that for a
long time I was accustomed to submit to every
kind of injustice simply for her sake. It was a
sad mistake. When it was practically discovered
that I would not defend myself, every kind of
indignity was put upon me, and my life was made
utterly miserable.

"Fortunately the strain was too great. One
day a big boy was annoying me, when it occurred
to my mind that existence under such conditions
was insupportable ; so I slipped off my *wooden*

shoe, and therewith suddenly gave that boy a blow on the seat of honour, which sent him sprawling on face and stomach in a convenient mass of mud and water. I shall never forget the burden that rolled off me at that moment. I never had a more heartfelt satisfaction than in witnessing the consternation of that contemporary. It proved to be a measure of peace also. From that time I was troubled by the boys no more."

Carlyle's mother died in 1853. Up to that time she carefully read all her great son's works, even his translation of "Wilhelm Meister," expressing, of course, decided disapproval of some of the very shady characters to be found in that extraordinary work. The "French Revolution" she read and re-read till she understood every line. As Carlyle resisted his mother's teaching of non-resistance, so he also disobeyed his father's rigid commands as to the books he should and should not read. He used to run away to the fields to enjoy Smollett's "Roderick Random." His delight in Smollett's works lasted to his last day. He said that nothing, even in Dante or out, excelled that passage in "Humphrey Clinker," where Humphrey goes into the smithy made for him in the old house, and whilst he is heating the iron, the poor woman who has lost her husband and is deranged, comes and talks to him as to her husband. "John, they told me you were dead. How glad I am you have come!" And Humphrey's tears fall down and bubble on the hot iron.

You will all remember that Sir Walter Scott had the same intense admiration for the broad humour and full-blooded humanity of Smollett, and that he read "Humphrey Clinker" almost on his death-bed.

Such were the parents of Carlyle. He often said that no noble man was born of a bad stock ; and would instance the Burns family, of whose attainments we are all aware.

Carlyle refused to enter the Church. He felt that his opinions, so broad and deep, could not be confined within the orthodox barriers. His grand mind and heart could not be controlled by theological cobwebs. He could not make up his mind to believe one thing and teach another. In matters of that kind, as he once said, "he supposed a man must be honest."

He wrote sixteen articles for the *Edinburgh Encyclopædia,* edited by his friend David Brewster. These articles I have read: the one on Montaigne is particularly good. They are written in quite ordinary diction, and contain nothing of his later mannerisms. They were written between the years 1820 and 1824. The translation of "Wilhelm Meister" appeared soon after. Jeffrey, the acute but very limited critic, who said that Wordsworth "would not do," wrote of this great work "that it was eminently absurd, puerile, incongruous, and affected. . . . Almost from beginning to end one flagrant offence against every principle of taste and every rule of composition." But then the great critic of the *Edinburgh Review*—a highly respectable quarterly, but always a little behind the time—kindly patronises the translator, " as one who has proved himself by his preface to be a person of talents, and by every part of the work to be no ordinary master of at least one of the languages with which he has to deal." The review finishes thus : " Many of the passages to which we have now alluded are executed with great talent, and we are very sensible are better worth extracting than those we have cited. But it is too late now to change our selections, and we can still less afford to add to them. On the whole, we close the book with some feeling of mollification toward its faults, and a disposition to abate, if possible, some part of the censure we were impelled to bestow on it at the beginning." This is the kind of absurdity men of talent produce—for Jeffrey was a man of talent—when they sit in judgment on a man of genius : where talent ends, genius begins.

Carlyle's delightful " Life of Schiller," one of the most fascinating biographies ever written, was translated by Goethe into German. It was published about the same time as " Wilhelm Meister." Carlyle, with iron resolution, continued his fight against fortune. He became tutor to Charles Buller. This was the turn of the tide.

We will now take up the thread of Carlyle's life after his marriage with Jane Welch, when they were settled at Craigenputtock Hill, where Emerson visited them. Of him Carlyle said : " Words cannot tell how I prize the old friendship formed here on Craigenputtock Hill, or how deeply I have felt in all he has written the same aspiring intelligence which shone about us when he came as a young man, and left with us a memory always cherished."

I will drop the thread of Emerson for a time in order to refer to one of the most striking tributes ever paid by one distinguished man to another : I mean that offered by John Tyndall to Thomas Carlyle, when the latter's statue was unveiled on the Chelsea Embankment. The professor began by a personal reminiscence. At the time of the Preston Guild of 1842 (Mr. Tyndall then being attached to the Ordnance Survey of that town) great distress existed, and in Lime Street the suffering operatives attacked the bakers' shops, and were fired upon by the military. Carlyle, then residing at Cheyne Row, was at work on " Past and Present," and the cry of the famishing weavers, coming to him from the North, brought forth the memorable appeal to Exeter Hall ; the appeal in which it was demanded that when Quashee over the seas *was* provided for, some attention should be paid to the " hunger-stricken, pallid, yellow-coloured, *free* labourers of Lancashire, Yorkshire, Buckinghamshire, and all other shires."

These were the first words of Carlyle, copied, as it were, into the Preston papers, which Professor Tyndall ever read, and, as he told his audience : " After the rattle of musketry and spatter of bullets among the weavers and spinners in Lime Street, they rang, I confess, with strange impressions in my ears." The professor, in glancing at the leading attributes of his character, said that Carlyle's defects—if such they were—could only have reference to the *distribution of his sympathy, not to its amount.* His pity was vast, and only his division of it between black and white could be called in question.

Carlyle he went on to describe as one who, day and night, for years brooded upon the condition of his toiling fellow-countrymen ; who saw the vanity of expecting political wisdom from intellectual ignorance ; whose influence went far beyond the sphere of politics ; who threw resolution and moral elevation into the hearts of the young ; who asserted the claims of duty and the dignity of work ; who was dynamic, not didactic—a spiritual force, " which warmed, moved, and invigorated, but which refused to be clipped into precepts "; and as one who hated sham, but whose spirit leaped to recognize true merit and manfulness.

Mr. Tyndall admitted that the bias of Carlyle's mind was certainly towards what might be called the military virtues, thinking, as he did, that they could not be dispensed with in the present temper of the world ; but added that though he bore about him the image and superscription of a great military commander, had he been a statesman, he would, at any moment, have accepted as the weapons of his warfare, instead of the sword and spear, the ploughshare and the pruning-hook of peaceful civic life.

Upon the subject of Carlyle's ethics the professor said : "Taking all that Science has done in the past, all that she has achieved in the present, and all that she is likely to compass in the future, will she at length have told us everything, rendering our knowledge of this universe rounded and complete? The answer is clear. After Science has completed her mission upon earth, the finite known will still be embraced by the infinite unknown. And this boundless contiguity of shade, by which our knowledge is hemmed in, will always tempt the exercise of belief and imagination. The human mind, in its structural and poetic capacity, can never be prevented from building its castles—on the rock or in the air, as the case may be—in this ultra-scientific region. Certainly the mind of Carlyle could not have

been prevented from doing so. Out of pure un-
intelligence he held that intelligence never could
have sprung, and so, at the heart of things, he
placed an intelligence—an energy which, to avoid
circuitous paraphrase, we call God.

" I am here repeating his own words to myself.
Every reader of his works will have recognized
the burning intensity of his conviction that this
universe is ruled by veracity and justice, which
are sure in the end to scorch and dissipate all
falsehood and wrong."

As to the charge so frequently made against
Carlyle, that he was the Apostle of Might, Professor Tyndall quoted the extract from "Chartism,"
in which the author pointed out that " might and
right do differ frightfully from hour to hour ; but
give them centuries to try it in, and they are found
in the end to be identical ; " and he concluded by an
expression of confidence that when all temporary
dust of misapprehension regarding Carlyle had
passed away, his massive figure will stand erect
and clear.

Before unveiling the statue, Mr. Tyndall ex-
pressed a wish that somewhere on the Thames
Embankment a memorial might be raised to a
man who loved Carlyle, and was by him beloved
to the end—" the loftiest, purest, and most
penetrating spirit that ever shone in American
literature—Ralph Waldo Emerson."

Before following this new link in my chain,

let me here introduce to your notice the following exquisite lines, which embody the religious ideas of Carlyle so beautifully and clearly presented by Professor Tyndall :—

> " There is no unbelief :
> Whoever plants a seed beneath the sod,
> And waits to see it push away the clod,
> He trusts in God.

> " Whoever says, when clouds are in the sky,
> ' Be patient, heart, light breaketh by-and-by,'
> Trusts the Most High.

> " Whoever sees, 'neath winter's field of snow,
> The silent harvest of the future grow,—
> God's power must know.

> " The heart that looks on when the eyelids close,
> And dares to live when life has only woes,
> God's comfort knows.

> " There is no unbelief :
> And day by day, and night, unconsciously,
> The *heart* lives by that faith the *lips* deny ;
> God knoweth why."

I think the judgment, the calm, analytical judgment, of a Tyndall on a Carlyle, to be priceless. No man was more capable of feeling the rough, vehement one-sidedness of Carlyle's judgment on some matters, which he never condescended to study, than Mr. Tyndall ; but with splendid receptivity, which I consider to be his great strength and the source of his intellectual

4

greatness, he felt to his heart's core the sublime
eloquence, the marvellous power of word-painting,
the infinite humour ; in short, the tremendous
and unique individuality of that literary Titan—
Thomas Carlyle.

Now, we will at last turn to that most vivid
description Emerson gives us in " English Traits "
of his first interview, the germ of a lifelong
friendship, with Carlyle.   This is the passage :
" From Edinburgh I went to the Highlands.
On my return, I came from Glasgow to Dum-
fries, and being intent on delivering a letter
which I had brought from Rome, inquired for
Craigenputtock.   It was a farm in Nithsdale,
in the parish of Dunscore, sixteen miles distant.
No public coach passed near it, so I took a
private carriage from the inn.   I found the
house amid desolate heathery hills, where the
lonely scholar nourished his mighty heart.

" Carlyle was a man from his youth, an author
who did not need to hide from his readers, and
as absolute a man of the world, unknown and
exiled on that hill farm, as if holding on his own
terms what is best in London.   He was tall and
gaunt, with a cliff-like brow, self-possessed, and
holding his extraordinary powers of conversation
in easy command ; clinging to his northern accent
with evident relish ; full of lively anecdote, and
with a streaming humour, which floated everything he looked upon. His talk, playfully exalting

the familiar objects, put the companion at once into an acquaintance with his *Lars and Lemurs*, and it was very pleasant to learn what was predestined to be a pretty mythology. Few were the objects and lonely the man,—'not a person to speak to within sixteen miles except the minister of Dunscore'; so that books inevitably made his topics. 'He had names of his own for all matters familiar to his discourse. *Blackwood's* was the 'sand magazine'; *Fraser's* nearer approach to possibility of life was the 'mud magazine'; a piece of road near by, that marked some foiled enterprise, was 'the grave of the last sixpence.' When too much praise of any genius annoyed him, he professed hugely to admire the talent shown by his pig. He had spent much time and contrivance in confining the poor beast to one enclosure in his pen, but pig, by great strokes of judgment, had found out how to let a board down, and had foiled him.

"For all that, he still thought man the most plastic little fellow in the planet. He worships a man that will manifest any truth to him.

"At one time he had inquired and read a good deal about America. Landor's principle was mere rebellion, and that, he feared, was the American principle. The best thing he knew of that country was, that in it a man can have meat for his labour. He had read in Stewart's book that when he inquired in a New York hotel for the boots, he had been shown across the street, and had found Mungo in his own house dining on roast turkey.

"We talked on books. Plato he does not read, and he disparaged Socrates; and, when pressed, persisted in making Mirabeau a hero. Gibbon he called the splendid bridge from the old world to the new. His own reading had been multifarious. 'Tristram Shandy' was one of his first books after 'Robinson Crusoe,' and Robertson's 'America' an early favourite. Rousseau's 'Confessions' had discovered to him that he was not a dunce; and it was now ten years since he had learned German, by the advice of a man who had told him he would find in that language what he wanted.

"He took despairing or satirical views of literature at this moment; recounted the incredible sums paid in one year by the great booksellers for puffing. [Emerson forgot to tell us how unknown that great art was in America.] Hence it comes that no newspaper is trusted now, no books are bought, and the booksellers are on the eve of bankruptcy. He still returned to English pauperism, the crowded country, the selfish abdication by public men of all that public persons should perform. 'Government should direct poor men what to do. Poor Irish folk come wandering over these moors. My dame makes it a rule to give to every son of

Adam bread to eat, and supplies his wants to
the next house. But here are thousands of acres
which might give them all meat, and nobody to
bid these poor Irish go to the moor and till it.
They burned the stacks, and so found a way to
force the rich people to attend to them.

"We went out to walk over long hills, and
looked at Criffel, then without his cap, and down
into Wordsworth's country. There we sat down,
and talked of the immortality of the soul. It
was not Carlyle's fault that we talked on that
subject, for he had the natural disinclination of
every nimble spirit to bruise itself against walls,
and did not like to place himself where no step
can be taken. But he was honest and true, and
cognizant of the subtle links that bind ages
together, and saw how every event affects all the
future.

"'Christ died on the tree; that built Dunscore
kirk yonder; that brought you and me together.
Time has only a relative existence.'

"He was already turning his eyes towards
London with a scholar's appreciation. 'London
is the heart of the world,' he said, 'wonderful
only from the mass of human beings.' He liked
the huge machine. Each keeps its own round.
The baker's boy brings muffins to the window
at a fixed hour every day, and that is all the
Londoner knows or wishes to know on the
subject. But it turned out good men."

I consider that one of the most interesting and
suggestive passages in literature.   How these
giants enjoyed their intellectual wrestlings one
with the other!   And this was the beginning of
an intimate friendship which never tired.   And
if, as we must admit, Carlyle's rugged vehemence
of temper introduced discord into their relations,
we must remember Mrs. Carlyle's pertinent
remark to some one who complimented her on
her husband's greatness : " Eh, man, what would
he have been if he had had a digestion ? "   There
is the key to Carlyle's faults of temper and
bitter prejudices.   His powers of expression
were so tremendous that he said in the heat
of conversational inspiration things that he
himself regretted deeply in his calmer moments.
Was it the act of a friend to put the worst things
said in the worst light ?

Carlyle, as you are aware, was born on December
4th, 1795, and died at Cheyne Row on February
5th, 1881.   The May number (1881) of *Scribner's
Magazine* contained a paper read partly by the
venerable sage Emerson on " Impressions of
Thomas Carlyle in 1848."   This was the last
tribute paid by Emerson to Carlyle, and is filled
with all that wisdom, wit, and subtle discrimina-
tion so characteristic of the greatest man America
has produced.

It must have been a very touching picture to
see Emerson, who was shortly to join his old

friend, referring to his daughter as to what he should read of the loose MSS. on his desk. It was a sight never to be forgotten by those present.

I must just submit a few passages of this swan-song of the great teacher.

"Nor can that decorum which is the idol of the Englishman, and in attaining which the Englishman exceeds all nations, win from Carlyle any obeisance. He is eaten up with indignation against such as desire to make a fair show in the flesh.

"Combined with this warfare on respectabilities, and, indeed, pointing all his satire, is the severity of his moral sentiment. In proportion to the peals of laughter amid which he strips the plumes of a pretender, and shows the lean hypocrisy to every vantage of ridicule, does he worship whatever enthusiasm, fortitude, love, or other sign of good nature is in man.

"There is nothing deeper in his constitution than his humour, than the considerate, condescending good nature with which he looks at every object in existence, as *a man might look at a mouse*. He feels that the perfection of health is sportiveness, and will not look grave even at dulness or tragedy.

"His guiding genius is his moral sense, his perception of the sole importance of truth and justice; but that is truth of character and not of catechisms.

"He says, 'There is properly no religion in

England. These idle nobles at Tattersall's—there is no word or work of serious purpose in them; they have this great lying Church : and life is a humbug.' He prefers Cambridge to Oxford, but he thinks Oxford and Cambridge education indurates the young men, as the Styx hardened Achilles, so that when they come forth of them they say, ' Now we are proof : we have gone through all the degrees, and are case-hardened against the veracities of the Universe ; nor man nor God can penetrate us."

*   *   *   *   *   *

A little further on, Emerson said : " He was very serious about the bad times ; he had seen this evil coming, but thought it would not come in his time. But now 'tis coming, and the only good he sees in it is the visible appearance of the Gods. He thinks it is the only question for wise men, instead of art, and fine fancies, and poetry, and such things,—*to address themselves to the problem of society.* This confusion is the inevitable end of such falsehood and nonsense as they have been embroiled with.

" Carlyle has, best of all men in England, kept the manly attitude in his time. He has stood for scholars, asking no scholar what he should say. Holding an honoured place in the best society, he has stood for the people, for the Chartist, for the pauper, intrepidly and scornfully teaching the nobles their peremptory duties.

" His errors of opinion are as nothing in com-
parison with this merit in my judgment.   This
aplomb cannot be mimicked ; it is the speaking
to the heart of the thing.   And in England, where
the morgue of aristocracy has very slowly admitted
scholars in society,—a very few houses in the high
circles being ever opened to them,—he has carried
himself erect, made himself a power confessed by
all men, and taught scholars their lofty duty.   *He
never feared the face of man.*"

> " Storm-god of the northern foam,
> Strong, wrought of rock that breasts and breaks the sea,
> And thunders back its thunder rhyme for rhyme,
> Answering as though to outroar the tides of time."

Now we will let Carlyle speak for himself.
My purpose is to select salient passages from his
writings, passages lighting up the dark depths of
his genius.

Carlyle's interest in and love for humanity was
deep and undeviating. This can be proved by
hundreds of passages from his works.   His very
scolding and apparent cynicism originated in the
disappointment he felt when he saw the concrete
man, and compared him with his dream of what
man could and should be.   He never spared himself, and he was " cruel to be kind " to others.
You will all remember this passage in which he
describes the workhouse of St. Ives:—

" I saw sitting on wooden benches, in front of

their Bastille, and within their ring-wall and its railings, some half-hundred or more of these men. Tall, robust figures, young mostly, or of middle age: of honest countenance, many of them thoughtful and even intelligent-looking men. They sat there, near by one another, but in a kind of torpor, and especially in a silence which was very striking. In silence; for, alas! what *word* was to be said? An earth all lying round crying, Come and till me, come and reap me; yet we sit here enchanted! In the eyes and brows of these men hung the gloomiest expression, not of anger, but grief and shame, and manifold inarticulate distress and weariness. They returned my glance with a glance that seemed to say, ' Do not look at us; we sit here enchanted, we know not why. The sun shines and the earth calls, and by the governing powers and impotences of this England we are forbidden to obey. It is impossible, they tell us!' There was something that reminded me of Dante's hell in the look of all this; and I rode swiftly away."

That strikes me as one of the most important passages of modern literature. He there places a problem before so-called statesmen, which they must either solve or be crushed by.

Then that unspeakably beautiful passage from the "Everlasting Yea," of which I can only quote a portion:—

" Foreshadows, call them rather fore-splendours, of that Truth, and Beginning of Truth, fell mysteriously over my soul. Sweeter than Day-spring to the shipwrecked in Nova Zembla ; ah ! like the mother's voice to her little child that strays bewildered, weeping, in unknown tumults ; like soft streamings of celestial music to my too-exasperated heart, came that Evangel ! The Universe is not dead and demoniacal, a charnel-house with spectres; but Godlike, and my Father's !

" With other eyes, too, could I now look upon my fellow-man : with an infinite Love, an infinite Pity. Poor, wandering, wayward man ! Art thou not tried, and beaten with stripes, even as I am ? Ever, whether thou bear the royal mantle or the beggar's gaberdine, art thou not so weary, so heavy-laden; and thy bed of rest is but a grave ? O my brother, my brother, why cannot I shelter thee in my bosom, and wipe away all tears from thy eyes !

" Truly, the din of many-voiced life, which in this solitude, with the mind's organ, I could hear, was no longer a maddening discord, but a melting one ; like inarticulate cries, and sobbings of a dumb creature, which in the ear of Heaven are prayers. The poor Earth, with her poor joys, was now my needy Mother, *not* my cruel Step-dame ; Man, with his so mad wants and so mean endeavours, had become dearer to me ; and even for his sufferings and his sins, I now first named him Brother. Thus was I standing in the porch of that 'Sanctuary of Sorrow' ; by strange, steep ways had I too been guided thither ; and ere long its sacred gates would open, and the 'Divine Depth of Sorrow' lie disclosed to me."

In that passage Carlyle opened to us the very deepest depth of his soul. And what a soul! What pity, deeper than tears, what thrilling, soul-piercing tenderness, pulses through it!

There is not an adagio of Mozart's or Beethoven's more unearthly in its sadness and solemn beauty.

Now let us touch another key, my object being to endeavour to show the compass of this extraordinary man, the deepest thinker and most loving heart of his time, in spite of the flabby twaddle and spiteful attacks of *dilettante* lotos-eaters and disappointed, snarling, would-be Carlyles.

"The Dandiacal Household : the Home of the Clothes-horse.

"A dressing-room splendidly furnished ; violet coloured curtains, chairs and ottomans of the same hue. Two full-length mirrors are placed, one on each side of a table, which supports the luxuries of a toilet. Several bottles of perfumes, arranged in a peculiar fashion, stand upon a smaller table of mother-of-pearl ; opposite to these are placed the appurtenances of lavation

richly wrought in frosted silver. A wardrobe of
Buhl is on the left, the doors of which, being
partly open, discover a profusion of clothes ;
shoes of a singularly small size monopolise the
lower shelves. Fronting the wardrobe a door
ajar gives some slight glimpse of a bath-room.
Folding doors in the background.

"Enter the Author, obsequiously preceded by
a French valet, in white silk jacket and cambric
apron."

So much for the Dandy, the "clothes-horse."
Now for the "Poor Irish Slave Household."
"The furniture of this Caravansera consisted
of a large iron pot, two oaken tables, two benches,
two chairs, and a potheen noggin. There was a
loft above (attainable by a ladder), in which the
inmates slept ; and the space below was divided by
a hurdle into two apartments ; the one for their
cow and pig, the other for themselves and guests.
On entering the house we discovered the family,
eleven in number, at dinner : the father sitting
at the top, the mother at the bottom, the children
on each side, of a large oaken board, which was
scooped out in the middle, like a trough, to
receive the contents of their pot of potatoes.
Little holes were cut at equal distances to contain
salt ; and a bowl of milk stood on the table : all
the luxuries of meat and beer, bread, knives and
dishes were dispensed with.

"The poor slave himself was broad-backed, black-browed, of great personal strength, and mouth from ear to ear. His wife was sun-browned, but a well-featured woman ; and his young ones, bare and chubby, had the appetites of ravens. Of their philosophical or religious tenets or observances, no notice or hint.

"Such," continues Carlyle, "are the two sects which, at this moment, divide the most unsettled portion of the British People ; and agitate that over-vexed country. To the eye of the political seer, their mutual relation, pregnant with the elements of discord and hostility, is far from con-soling.   These two principles of Dandiacal Self-Worship or Demon-Worship, and Poor-Slavish or Drudgical Earth-Worship, or whatever the same Drudgism may be, do as yet indeed manifest themselves under distant and nowise considerable shapes : nevertheless, in their roots and subter-ranean ramifications, they extend through the entire structure of Society, and work unweariedly in the secret depths of English national existence ; striving to separate and isolate it into two con-tradictory, uncommunicating masses."

I cannot pursue this passage to the end, but will conclude with the following summing up :—

"I might call them two boundless, and indeed unexampled electric machines (turned by the 'Machinery of Society'), with batteries of opposite quality ; Drudgism the Negative, Dandyism the

Positive : one attracts hourly towards it and appropriates all the Positive Electricity of the nation (namely, the Money thereof) ; the other is equally busy with the Negative (that is to say, the Hunger), *which is equally potent.* Hitherto you see only partial transient sparkles and sputters ; but wait a little, till the entire nation is in an electric state—till your whole vital Electricity, no longer healthfully neutral, is cut into insulated portions of Positive and Negative (of Money and Hunger), and stands there bottled up in two World Batteries ! The stirring of a child's finger brings the two together ; and then— *What then ? The* **earth** *is but shivered into* **impalpable** *smoke by that Doom's thunder-peal ;* **the Sun misses one of** *his Planets in space, and thenceforth* **there are no** *eclipses of the Moon.*"

That passage recalls Carlyle's weighty words : " One should see before one pretends to oversee."

How many shallow people, who, if they devoted the whole of their small minds and smaller hearts—for to understand a real genius it is as necessary to use the heart as the brain—would only be able to comprehend the mere fringe of a profound writer like Carlyle, yet give their adverse verdict about him with the most fatuous complacency. Why, half a dozen of Carlyle's ideas would crack their egg-shells of heads ! The passage just quoted, on Dandies and Drudges, as you will doubtless remember, appeared in

"Sartor Resartus," published in 1831, nearly sixty years ago. And it has taken all that time to enable ordinary people to just obtain a glimmering notion of what Carlyle boldly and trenchantly stated more than half a century ago.

Now we will turn to the sweet middle tones of Carlyle's genius.

The following passage on musical or rhythmical utterance is, in my humble opinion, exquisite and strong :—

"Nevertheless, you will say, there must be a difference between true Poetry and true speech not poetical: what is the difference? On this point many things have been written, especially by late German Critics, some of which are not very intelligible at first. They say, for example, that the Poet has an *infinitude* in him ; communicates an *Unendlichkeit*, a certain character of *infinitude*, to whatsoever he delineates.

"This, though not very precise, yet on so vague a matter is worth remembering: if well meditated, some meaning will gradually be found in it. For my own part, I find considerable meaning in the old vulgar distinction of Poetry being *metrical*, having music in it, being a Song.

"Truly, if pressed to give a definition, one might say this as soon as anything else. If your delineation be authentically *musical*—musical not in word only, but in heart and substance, in all the thoughts and utterances of it, in the whole conception of it—then it will be poetical ; if not, not. Musical : how much lies in that ! A musical thought is one spoken by a mind that has penetrated into the inmost heart of the thing ; detected the inmost mystery of it, namely the *melody* that lies hidden in it ; the inward harmony of coherence which is its soul, whereby it exists, and has a right to be here in this world. All inmost things, we may say, are melodious ; naturally utter themselves in song. The meaning of song goes deep. Who is there that, in logical words, can express the effect music has on us? A kind of inarticulate, unfathomable speech, which leads to the edge of the Infinite, and lets us for moments gaze into that ! Nay, all speech, even the commonest speech, has something of song in it ; not a parish in the world but has its parish-accent—the rhythm or *tune* to which the people there *sing* what they have to say ! Accent is a kind of chanting; all men have accent of their own, though they only *notice* that of others.

" Observe, too, how all passionate language does of itself become musical,—with a finer music than the mere accent ; the speech of a man even in zealous anger becomes a chant, a song. All deep things are Song. It seems somehow the very central essence of us, Song ; as if all the rest were but wrappings and hulls : the primal element of us ; of us, and of all things. The Greeks fabled of Sphere-

Harmonies : it was the feeling they had of the inner structure of Nature : that the soul of all her voices and utterances was perfect music. Poetry, therefore, we call Musical Thought. The Poet is he who thinks in that manner. At bottom, it turns still on power of intellect ; it is a man's sincerity and depth of vision that makes him a Poet. See deep enough, and you see musically ; the heart of Nature being everywhere music, if you can only reach it."

That passage conducts one step by step to the starry heights of poetry. What clearness, and what beauty ! It reminds one of Mendelssohn saying, " If music could be described by words, I would not compose." It suggests more than it utters.

Carlyle never rests on the surface of any subject; that is why superficial people don't like him. His method is to penetrate to the depths, to what he calls the tap-root. And when he is there, he sees the connection of one root with another. Where talent sees differences genius sees connection. The talented man talks about this link of the chain or the other ; the man of genius welds them together, making a beautiful chain, in which every link is placed in proportion to its importance. Men of talent very naturally dislike men of genius ; they don't like to have their rushlights extinguished by the burning, solar rays of genius.

After the passage last quoted, we cannot descend to anything less exalted and beautiful. We will now hear what our great seer and teacher said on the poetry of poetry—Religion.

"There is no Church, sayest thou? The voice of prophecy has gone dumb? This is even what I dispute : but in any case, hast thou not still preaching enough? A preaching Friar settles himself in every village, and builds a pulpit, which he calls a newspaper. Therefrom he preaches what most momentous doctrine is in him, for man's salvation; and dost not thou listen, and believe? Look well, thou seest everywhere a new Clergy of the Mendicant Orders some barefoot, some almost barebacked, fashion itself into shape, and teach and preach, zealously enough, for copper alms and the love of God. These break in pieces the ancient idols ; and, though themselves too often reprobate, as idol-breakers are wont to be, make out the site for new Churches, where the true God-ordained, that are to follow, may find audience, and minister. Said I not, Before the old skin was shed, the new had formed itself beneath it ?

"But is there no Religion? reiterates the Professor. Fool ! I tell thee, there is. Hast thou well considered all that lies in this immense froth ocean we name Literature ? Fragments of genuine Church Homiletic lie scattered there, which time will assort : nay, fractions even of a

Liturgy could I point out. And knowest thou no Prophet, even in the vesture, environment, and dialect of this age? None to whom the Godlike had revealed itself, through all meanest and highest forms of the common ; and by him had been again prophetically revealed : in whose inspired melody, even in these rag-gathering and rag-burning days, Man's Life again begins, were it but afar off, to be Divine? Knowest thou none such? I know him, and name him—Goethe.

" But thou as yet standest in no Temple ; joinest in no Psalm-worship ; feelest well that, where is no ministering Priest, the people perish? Be of comfort ! *Thou art not alone, if thou have Faith.* Spake we not of a Communion of Saints, unseen, yet not unreal, accompanying and brotherlike embracing thee, so thou be worthy ?

" Their heroic sufferings rise up melodiously together to Heaven, out of all lands, and out of all times, as a sacred *Miserere* ; their heroic Actions also, as a boundless everlasting Psalm of Triumph. Neither say that thou hast now no Symbol of the Godlike. Is not God's universe a Symbol of the Godlike? Is not Immensity a Temple? Is not Man's History a perpetual Evangel?

" Listen, and for organ music thou wilt ever, as of old, hear the Morning Stars sing together.

" Master, who savedst others, that thyself
Thou couldst not save by some is made thy crime,—
Oh, not by us !   For we were call'd by thee,
And from thy strife a battle-cry arose
Which pierced thy heart, but temper'd ours, and made
Us live new lives as soldiers, conquerors, *men*.

" Shall we arraign the strife, and name defeat
Repulses, wounds, that were *our victory* ?
Nay, master, nay !   Thy maims, thy scars, thy cries,
Though they distort thee, sacred are to us,
As bitter losses which thou mad'st *our gain*.

" Round thy dishonour'd grave we come, we press,
And o'er the stains which traitorous hands laid bare
Our tears are flowing ; and where once was heard
The *slanderer's tongue*, a low deep murmur sounds
Thy blessing, Carlyle, in unnumbered hearts."

NOTE.

Carlyle thus described Disraeli in 1867, before the purchase of the Suez Canal shares, before the Afghan and Zulu wars, before annexing the Transvaal and taking Cyprus, before establishing the Dual Control, before he got £6,000,000 to prepare for war with Russia, and before he egged on France to take Tunis.   I don't want to be hard on the dear—very dear—departed, so I will stop here.   But this is how Carlyle painted the great medicine-man :—

" A superlative Hebrew conjuror, spell-binding all the great lords, great parties, grea   interests of England, to his hand in this manner, and leading them by the nose, like helpless, mesmerised somnambulant cattle.   This, too, I suppose we have deserved.   The end of our poor old England to be, not a tearful tragedy, but an ignominious farce as well ! "

In contrast to that, listen to what the once mighty
Times said of the same great man after the extraordinary
absurdity of Primrose Day :—

"Benjamin Disraeli was the most delightful little
fellow in the world when he had barely emerged from
infancy ; and he never became otherwise."

He was, according to that great authority, the *Times*,
a gentle, simple, get-into-the-shade sort of a human
primrose.

THE EARL AND THE PRIMROSE.

" Little rustic flower, in thee
  Emblem true of Ben we see,
  Artless, modest (such was he),
  Full of sweet simplicity,
  Softly, innocently wild,
  Nature's unassuming child.
  Hadst thou not before been known,
  By his tomb thou must have grown,
  And some new Ovid sing of this
  Lovely metamorphosis.
  Fragrant, humble, tender blossom,
  Fit for every Tory bosom."

Now listen to what Carlyle said of Mr. Gladstone, in
a letter to Emerson, dated February 8th, 1839 :—

"One of the strangest things about the 'New England
Orations' (Emerson's) is a fact I have heard, that a certain
Mr. Gladstone, an Oxford crack scholar, Tory M.P., and
devout Churchman, of great talent and hope, has contrived to insert a piece of you in a work of his own on
Church and State, which makes some figure at present !
I know him for a solid, serious, silent-minded man ; but
how, with his Coleridge shovel-hattism, he has contrived
to relate himself to *you*—there is the mystery.   True
men of all creeds, it would seem, are brothers."

III.

RALPH WALDO EMERSON.

When so clear and far-shining a star as Emerson fades out, one, at first, feels numbed : it takes some time to realise the loss sustained.

We forget in the whirl of vulgar cares and interests the great intellectual benefactors of humanity. Some of us have absorbed more or less of their teaching, and feel a vague love and reverence for the teacher. Then one morning one reads in the newspaper that the great and good man is ill—that the bright light is becoming dim ; and a few days later one is shocked to learn that it has gone out for ever—that the intellectual fire which lit the world with its lambent flame is extinguished. We know how difficult it is for ordinary people to keep alive a spark of inner light, and yet this sublime old man, in spite of the obstacles, worries, and peddling cares of poor human nature, not only kept bright the inner light of his own soul, but assisted millions to do the same.

What we admire in Emerson is not only the

intellectual elevation, but the moral purity and simple childlike goodness and sweetness of the man. Success did not spoil him, although it came very early. When I say success, I don't mean what the vulgar call success. The success valued by a man like Emerson was an extended power to do good. It did not consist in possessing houses, carriages, and servants. But when he knew that the intellectual and moral light which emanated from him was lighting up the best hearts, brains, and consciences of the English-speaking people, he had his exceeding great reward. And this gifted man looked upon every other man, woman and child as interesting and lovable. He listened with an unfailing courtesy to the stuttering speech of uncultivated people, hoping beneath the stumbling *words* to find some *idea* worthy of attention. And I believe he was often rewarded. For education, in which I have a most potent belief, although it develops the large brain, often crushes the small grain of originality which exists in the small one. The small jewel will not bear much cutting, the large one will. You make the most of the latter, the former you reduce to dust.

All my readers have enjoyed the raciness and wit of Emerson ; and, I believe, a great part of those rare qualities were gained by his power of opening the hearts and mouths of the people : the rough, the uncouth, but, in this sophisticated age, when ordinary respectable people are, on the surface, nearly as much alike as Birmingham buttons, the study of the people, to a man who wishes to understand the real grit and power of human nature, is altogether priceless.

Emerson lived a beautifully simple life. He was ready to listen to everybody; and did so with infinite benefit to his head and heart, not to mention ours. Nothing is so easy for a cultivated man to do as to freeze into silence uncultivated people. But I don't think you will find any author worth reading who adopted that form of intellectual and moral suicide.

The peculiar note of Emerson's style is its elevation and simplicity. He did not think of pleasing or displeasing any one; and therefore succeeded in delighting every one worth pleasing. I need scarcely say that so soon as a man of genius begins to think of pleasing this editor or the other by what he writes, it is all over with him as a teacher : and a good thing too. I want to know, and you want to know, and every one with any intellectual or moral earnestness wants to know, exactly what a man of genius thinks and feels about this, that, and the other; and not what some publisher or editor, who usually is not a man of genius, thinks will please the vulgar public.

A man who thinks of the success of his writing, and not of his writing only, may gain a superficial success. He may be noticed by the *Times*, and even worse papers, but he never gains, and never deserves to gain, a hold on the brains and hearts of mankind.

It is not by pleasing the vulgar that a man succeeds. It is by pleasing the wise and discriminating, who dictate to the vulgar what to admire.

Genius can only be thoroughly appreciated by genius. A man can only be really judged by his peers. But still we little people may pick up some little thoughts and ideas, suitable to our size, and, if we are strong enough, carry them away. But when some puny whipster, who can scarcely reach to the knees of an intellectual giant like Emerson, attempts to measure, weigh, and dissect him, one would be very angry, were it not too preposterously absurd, and the anger ends in a hearty laugh. The flea finding fault with the lion, on which it lives, is too absurd.

"A lion was once slightly bit by a flea:
'Twas the flea's way of saying, 'Take notice of me!'"

But as a rule lions don't take notice ; asses in lions' skins do. But I will do this justice to the critics : they appear to have given Emerson a wide berth.

They looked upon him as too far gone. Not even their wonderful teaching powers could benefit such a hopeless case. With him they lost their Latin. What a blessing! " *The lion never lost so much time as when he took lessons from the ape.*" Emerson, I think, never lost much time in that way. He went on his own solitary intellectual path—the higher the path the more solitary—disregarding the praise or the blame of foolish people. That wise conduct was the root of his power and strength.

Now I must say a word about one of the most salient features in Emerson's character. I mean his unfailing goodness. No man was less goody, and no man was more truly good. Thackeray once said, although a better man than he never lived, that it was a great pity good people were so stupid. Now, I think it is a great blessing that bad people are so stupid. A bad heart, in my humble opinion, is often accompanied by a worse head. I think Carlyle was of opinion that the grand quality in literature and art is the moral quality. I think it is the salt of literature and art. People must love the truth and the right very ardently to find their way to them through the labyrinth of sophistries and lies which hide them from the lukewarm.

And, although we may not think so, a love of truth for its own sake is very rare. I think that was the particular and individual note of Emerson's genius. He did not trouble himself as to the effect of what he said on theological dogmas, or on social and political opinion; but said exactly, and in a clear and beautiful way, what *he* thought and felt on matters which appeared to him to be important. I think you will agree with me, that that is the one priceless quality in a teacher. Ninety-nine writers out of a hundred, highly respectable and talented men, writers of those wonderful productions called leading articles—though why they are called *leading* articles I am at a loss to understand—don't appear to me to care one farthing for the truth of what they write, but, according to the politics of their paper, attack or praise this man and the other. The same kind of thing obtains in many other cases, where the writing is larger in bulk, but where the same want of earnestness is felt. If a man speaks to you, and utters the inmost feelings of his nature, there is something to be learnt from him. But if he repeats to you, in a lame and impotent way, a lame and impotent leading article or speech, what help is there in that?

So that if the speech of an ordinary man, if earnest and true, is worth listening to, what must the speech of a man of the intellectual and moral calibre of Emerson be worth? Who can say? I believe it to be beyond the power of words to utter.

He looked into his heart and wrote. But he was always, by study and observation, enriching his heart and brain. Because, in my humble opinion, if a man is to speak or write much, he must study and think more, or his speech and writing soon tire. Dr. Johnson, in his blunt way, once said, "I despise the man who talks more than he reads." Dr. Johnson talked much, but he talked well, because he read and thought more.

And that, I think, accounts, in great measure, for what is called the fickleness of the public. An author produces a work that gives great promise of future excellence. The public is eager to see this promise fulfilled. A new work is produced in a great hurry; the public is disappointed, and the book fails. Whose fault is that? I think the careless author's. Emerson was never in a hurry to publish. He never tired of taking pains; and the public, therefore, never tired of him. You all know Sheridan said that easy writing is —— hard reading.

Emerson had the instincts, if I may use the term, of the writer and the orator. He could not help being picturesque and striking. It was as natural for Emerson to be brilliant and eloquent as for Dr. Dryasdust to be dull and pedantic. He was a man of the greatest candour and simplicity, but as a writer and speaker he had the most extraordinary tact and subtlety. No one capable of understanding him could fail to be carried away by the personal fascination of his style and manner.

Style is the man, a witty Frenchman said.

The only bad style is the dull style ; and it is perfectly natural to a dull man. But, after all, the only style worth anything is that which grows out of a man's nature, as individual and peculiar as his nose and fingers. When a man imitates another man's style he commits suicide as a writer. When one reads a friend's writing one ought to be able to say, No one could do that but so-and-so ; his individuality stamps every line. Compare for one moment the style of Emerson with that of Wendell Holmes. The style of one represents him as much as the style of the other represents that other. The style of Emerson is manly, clear, deep, and direct ; full of *verve* and poetical energy : it reflects the writer. The style of Wendell Holmes is subtle, charming, full of opalescent colour, witty, brilliant, and caustic : it also reflects the author.

The best thing I ever heard about style is this : understand thoroughly what you want to say, and say it in the fewest possible words. I apprehend that Emerson was of that opinion. We are not all bound to speak and write in one style. In fact, we are bound not to do so. In addition, we can't. But if we have anything to say, we are bound to respect the public suffi- ciently to say what we think and feel to the best of our poor ability. The public will very soon let a man know whether his intellectual wares suit the market or not.

Now I have given you my opinion on Emerson's character and genius, I will endeavour to prove from his works that my opinion is endorsed by them; and I will not only quote his prose —which, I think, is winged prose—but will also quote two or three of his most delicate, musical, and profoundly philosophical poems.

My only desire is to make you all love and reverence one of the noblest, purest, and loftiest men who ever lived for the purpose, it seems to me, of teaching man that he was made in the image of his Maker!

As we are naturally interested in ourselves, let me first quote some passages from " English Traits."

You, of course, have read that wise and witty book, but those who have studied it most will most enjoy hearing quotations from it. And if there are any of my readers who have not read it, perhaps my selections may induce them to do so. I expect, then, to be ever afterwards remembered as the man who first made them read Emerson.

George Dawson introduced me to Emerson's works. I admired and loved George Dawson, to whom I owe a great debt for intellectual stimulus; and not the least part of that debt arises from the fact that it was through him that I first studied Emerson.

I ought to mention here that Emerson was

born at Boston in 1803 ; that he graduated at
Harvard in 1821 ; that he published " Literary
Ethics " in 1838; " Man, the Reformer " in 1841 ;
" Representative Men " and " English Traits " in
1856 ; the " Conduct of Life " in 1860 ; that he
was a very tall man, with a fine, intellectual
face ; that he thoroughly believed in himself, and
that he had the power of making others do the
same, which is, after all, the one crucial test
of genius.

The following is Emerson's definition of the
English character :—

" The English composite character betrays a
mixed origin.   Everything English is a fusion of
distant and antagonistic elements.   The language
is mixed ; the names of men are of different
nations,—three languages, three or four nations ;—
the currents of thought are counter : contemplation and practical skill ; active intellect and dead
conservatism ; worldwide enterprise and devoted
use and wont ; aggressive freedom and hospitable
law, with bitter class legislation ; a people scattered by their wars and affairs over the whole
earth, and homesick to a man ; a country of extremes,—dukes and chartists, Bishops of Durham
and naked heathen colliers ;—nothing can be
praised in it without damning, and nothing
denounced without salvos of cordial praise."

That is tolerably clear and to the point for a
writer of intellectual moonshine, as Emerson has

been described by writers who know as much about him as a donkey knows about Beethoven. The opinion of a donkey is valuable—on thistles.

Now for another passage from the same work :

"They [the English] are rather manly than warlike. When the war is over, the mask falls from the affectionate and domestic tastes, which makes them women in kindness. This union of qualities is fabled in their national legend of 'Beauty and the Beast'; or, long before, in the Greek legend of 'Hermaphrodite.'

"The two sexes are co-present in the English mind. I apply to Britannia, queen of seas and colonies, the words in which her latest novelist portrays his heroine : 'She is as mild as she is game, and as game as she is mild.' The English delight in the antagonism which combines in one person the extremes of courage and tenderness. Nelson, dying at Trafalgar, sends his love to Lord Collingwood, and, like an innocent school-boy that goes to bed, says, 'Kiss me, Hardy,' and turns to sleep. Lord Collingwood, his comrade, was of a nature the most affectionate and domestic. Admiral Rodney's figure approached to delicacy and effeminacy, and he declared himself very sensible to fear, which he surmounted only by considerations of honour and public duty.

"Clarendon says the Duke of Buckingham was so modest and gentle, that some courtiers attempted to put affronts on him, until they found

that this modesty and effeminacy was only a
mask for the most terrible determination. And
Sir James Parry said, the other day, of Sir John
Franklin, that ' if he found Wellington Sound
open, he explored it ; for he was a man who never
turned his back on a danger, yet of that tenderness, that he would not brush away a mosquito.'
Even for their highwaymen the same virtue is
claimed ; and Robin Hood comes described to us
as *mitissimus prædonum*, the gentlest thief.

" But they know where their war-dogs lie.
Cromwell, Blake, Marlborough, Chatham, Nelson,
and Wellington are not to be trifled with, and
the brutal strength which lies at the bottom of
society, the animal ferocity of the quays and
cockpits, the bullies and the costermongers of
Shoreditch, Seven Dials, and Spitalfields, 'they
know how to wake up.' "

That passage is written by a man with some
of the bull-dog tenacity and force of the old sea-
dogs in his nature, I think. Not much " bottled
moonshine " about that, I apprehend.

" The island (England) was renowned in antiquity for its breed of mastiffs, so fierce that,
when their teeth were set, you must cut their
heads off to part them.

" The man was like his dog. The people have
that nervous bilious temperament, which is known
by medical men to resist every means employed
to make its possessor subservient to the will of

others. The English game is main force to main force, the planting of foot to foot, fair play and open field,—a rough tug without trick or dodging, till one or both come to pieces. King Ethelwald spoke the language of his race when he planted himself at Wimborne, and said, '*He would do one of two things, or there live, or there lie.*' They hate craft and subtlety. They neither waylay, nor assassinate ; and, when they have pounded each other to a poultice, they will shake hands and be friends for the remainder of their lives."

I consider that passage is as vigorous and Teutonic in tone as anything in Ben Jonson, Fielding, Smollett, or Carlyle.

" The Normans came out of France into England worse men than they went into it, one hundred and sixty years before. They had lost their own language, and learned the Romance or barbarous Latin of the Gauls ; and had acquired, with the language, all the vices it had names for. The Conquest has obtained in the chronicles the name of the ' Memory of Sorrow.' Twenty thousand thieves landed at Hastings. These founders of the House of Lords were greedy and ferocious pirates. They were all alike : they took everything they could carry ; they burned, harried, violated, tortured, and killed, until everything English was brought to the verge of ruin. Such, however, is the illusion of antiquity and wealth, that decent and dignified men now existing boast their descent, from these filthy thieves, who showed a far juster conviction of their own merits, by assuming for their types the swine, goat, jackal, leopard, wolf, and snake, which they severally resembled."

I think that will do for a specimen of the holy indignation that burned in the heart of Emerson against aristocratic pretensions and absurd pride.

I have given the deep bass of Emerson's harmony ; I will now proceed with the treble melody.

Emerson taught no exact system of philosophy, thank heaven ! But if philosophy means a love of wisdom, he was a philosopher. Emerson saw, felt, and thought ; and, from time to time, gave the public the results. He did not try to be consistent. He only endeavoured to be true. What he thought on Monday he wrote or said. But that did not prevent him telling you, next Saturday, that he thought, through new knowledge, something quite different. How many men dare to utter their real thoughts ? Emerson did not try to think for you ; he endeavoured to make you think for yourself. He had no cut-and-dried formulæ ; he did not believe in them. He did for the mind what the sea air does for the body— braced it. Emerson raised you, or tried to raise you, to a height from which you could look down upon the intellectual fog in which most

of us live ; and enabled you to see, and tried
to make you love, the pure white light of first
principles.

" Divine philosophy ! not harsh and crabbed,
    As dull fools suppose, but musical as is Apollo's lute ;
    And a perpetual feast of nectared sweets, where no
        dull surfeit waits."

The first passage I will quote is from Emerson's
essay on Nature :—

" To go into solitude a man needs to retire as
much from his chamber as from society. I am
not solitary while I read and write, though
nobody is with me. But if a man would be
alone, let him look at the stars. The rays that
come from those heavenly worlds will separate
between him and vulgar things. One might
think the atmosphere was made transparent with
this design, to give man, in the heavenly bodies,
the perpetual presence of the sublime. Seen in
the streets of cities, how great they are ! If the
stars should appear one night in a thousand years,
how men would believe and adore, and preserve
for many generations the remembrance of the city
of God which had been shown ! But every night
come out those preachers of beauty, and light the
universe with their admonishing smile.

" The stars awaken a certain reverence, because,
though always present, they are always inacces-
sible ; but all natural objects make a kindred

impression when 'the mind is open to their influence. Nature never wears a mean appearance.
Neither does the wisest man extort all her secret,
and lose his curiosity by finding out all her perfection. Nature never becomes a toy to a wise spirit.
The flowers, the animals, the mountains, reflected
all the wisdom of his best hour, as much as they
had delighted the simplicity of his childhood.
To speak truly, few adult persons can see Nature.
Most persons do not see the sun ; at least, they
have a very superficial seeing. The sun illumi-
nates only the eye of the man, but shines into
the eye and heart of the child. The lover of
Nature is he whose inward and outward senses
are still truly adjusted to each other ; and who
has retained the spirit of infancy even into the
era of manhood. His intercourse with heaven
and earth becomes part of his daily food. In
the presence of Nature a wild delight runs
through the man, in spite of real sorrows. Nature
says—He is my creature ; and maugre all his
impertinent griefs, he shall be glad with me.

"Not the sun or the summer alone, but every
hour and season, yields its tribute of delight ;
for every hour and change corresponds to and
authorises a different state of the mind, from
breathless noon to grimmest midnight. Nature
is a setting that fits equally well a comic or a
mourning piece. In good health the air is a
cordial of incredible virtue. Crossing a bare

common, in snow puddles, at twilight, under a
clouded sky, without having in my thoughts an
occurrence of special good fortune, I have enjoyed
a perfect exhilaration. Almost I fear to think
how glad I am. In the woods, too, he casts off
his years as the snake his slough, and, at what
period soever of life, is always a child. In the
woods is perpetual youth. Within these planta-
tions of God decorum and sanctity reign ; a
perennial festival is dressed, and the guest sees
not how he should tire of them in a thousand
years. In the woods we return to reason and
faith. There I feel that nothing can befall me
in life,—no disgrace, no calamity (leaving me
my eyes), which Nature cannot repair. Standing
on the bare ground, my head bathed by the
blithe air, and uplifted into infinite space, all
mean egotism vanishes. I become a transparent
eyeball. I am nothing. I see all. The currents
of the Universal Being circulate through me ; I
am part and particle of God. The name of the
nearest friend sounds then foreign and accidental.
To be brothers, to be acquaintances, master or
servant, is then a trifle and a disturbance. I am
the lover of uncontained and immortal beauty.
In the wilderness I find something more dear
and connate than in streets and villages. In the
tranquil landscape, and especially in the distant
line of the horizon, man beholds somewhat as
beautiful as his own nature."

The following passage on "Beauty" is from the same essay :—

" The presence of a higher, namely, of the spiritual element, is essential to its perfection. The high and Divine beauty which can be loved without effeminacy, is that which is found in combination with the human will, and never separate. Beauty is the mark God sets upon virtue. [Goethe said, "The Beautiful contained the Good."] Every natural action is graceful. Every heroic act is also decent, and causes the place and the bystanders to shine. We are taught by great actions that the universe is the property of every individual in it. Every rational creature has all nature for his dowry and estate. It is his, if he will. He may divest himself of it; he may creep into a corner, and abdicate his kingdom, as most men do, but he is entitled to the world by his constitution. In proportion to the energy of his thought and will, he takes up the world into himself. 'All these things for which we plough, build, or sail, obey virtue,' said an ancient historian. 'The winds and waves,' said Gibbon, 'are always on the side of the ablest navigators.' So are the sun and moon and all the stars of heaven. When a noble act is done,—perchance in a scene of great natural beauty,—when Leonidas and his three hundred martyrs consume one day in dying, and sun and moon come each and look at them once

in the steep defile of Thermopylæ ; when Arnold
Winckelried, in the high Alps, under the shadow
of the avalanche, gathers in his side a sheaf of
Austrian spears to break the line for his com-
rades,—are not these heroes entitled to add the
beauty of the scene to the beauty of the deed ?
When the bark of Columbus nears the shores
of America,—before it, the beach lined with
savages, fleeing out of all their huts of cane, the
sea behind, and all the purple mountains of the
Indian Archipelago around,— can we separate the
man from the living picture ? Does not the New
World clothe his form with her palm groves and
savannahs as fit drapery ? Ever does natural
beauty steal in like air, and envelop great actions.
When Sir Harry Vane was dragged up the
Tower Hill, sitting on a sled, to suffer death,
as the champion of the English laws, one of the
multitude cried out to him, ' You never sat on so
glorious a seat.'

"Charles II., to intimidate the citizens of
London, caused the patriot, Lord Russell, to be
drawn in an open coach, through the principal
streets of the city, on his way to the scaffold.
' But,' to use the simple narrative of his bio-
grapher, ' the multitude thought they saw Liberty
and Virtue sitting by his side.'

" In private places, among sordid objects, an act
of truth or heroism seems at once to draw to
itself the sky as its temple, the sun as its candle.

Nature stretches forth her arms to embrace man,
only let his thoughts be of equal greatness.
Willingly does she follow his steps with the rose
and the violet, and bend her lines of grandeur
and grace to the decoration of her darling child.
Only let his thoughts be of equal scope, and the
frame will suit the picture. A virtuous man is
in unison with her works, and makes the central
figure of the visible sphere. Homer, Pindar,
Socrates, Phocion, associate themselves fitly in
our memory with the whole geography and
climate of Greece. The visible heavens and
earth sympathise with Jesus. And in common
life, whosoever has seen a person of powerful
character and happy genius, will have remarked
how easily he took all things along with him,—
the persons, the opinions, and the day, and Nature
became ancillary to a man.

"The problem of restoring to the world original
and eternal beauty is solved by the redemption
of the soul. The ruin or the blank that we see
when we look at Nature is in our own eye. The
axis of vision is not coincident with the axis of
things, and so they appear not transparent, but
opaque. The reason why the world lacks unity,
and lies broken and in heaps, is, because man is
disunited with himself."

One other profound passage from this masterpiece :—

"There are innocent men who worship God

after the tradition of their fathers, but their sense of duty has not yet extended to the use of all their faculties. And there are naturalists, but they freeze their subject under the wintry light of the understanding."

Such writing as that is above ordinary criticism. It either raises the reader to a height of intellectual exaltation or it does not. No man should dare to patronise Emerson : not even a Shakespeare.

I make no apology for introducing here Mr. Lowell's parallel between Emerson and Carlyle, which is as wise, witty, and discriminating as anything written by that weighty and brilliant writer.

"There are persons mole-blind to the soul's make and
    style,
Who insist on a likeness 'twixt him and Carlyle.
To compare him with Plato would be vastly fairer :
Carlyle's the more burly, but E. is the rarer.
He sees fewer objects, but clearlier, truelier,
If C.'s as original, E.'s more peculiar.
That he's more of a man, you might say of the one ;
Of the other, he's more of an Emerson.
C.'s the Titan, as shaggy of mind as of limb ;
E.'s the clear-eyed Olympian, rapid and slim ;
The one's two-thirds Norseman, the other half Greek,
Where the one's most abounding, the other's to seek ;
C.'s generals require to be seen in the mass,
E.'s specialties gain if enlarged by the glass ;
C. gives Nature and God his own fits of the blues,
And rims common-sense things with mystical hues ;
E. sits in a mystery calm and intense,
And looks coolly round him with sharp common-sense ;

C. shows you how everyday matters unite
With the dim trans-diurnal recesses of night ;
While E., in a plain, preternatural way,
Makes mysteries matters of mere every day.
C. draws all his characters quite *à la* Fuseli,—
He don't sketch their bundles of muscles and thews silly,
But he paints with a brush so untamed and profuse,
They seem nothing but bundles of muscles and thews ;
E. is rather like Flaxman, lines straight and severe,
And a colourless outline, but full, round, and clear ;—
To the men he thinks worthy he frankly accords
The design of a white marble statue in words.
C. labours to get at the centre, and then
Take a reckoning from there of his actions and men ;
E. calmly assumes the said centre is granted,
And, given himself, has whatever is wanted."

I trust my quotations are not tiring you. My great difficulty has been to choose them, and my greatest trouble to curtail them. I have been unable to touch, in this paper, on his grand work, "Representative Men," which, in my humble opinion, is, for its power of intellectual stimulation, of the greatest possible value. I cannot withhold the following powerful passage on the thinker.

In speaking of the duties of a thinker, Emerson said :—

"They are such as become Man—Thinking. They may all be comprised in *self-trust*. The office of the scholar is to cheer, to raise, and to guide men, by showing them facts and appearances. He plies the slow, unhonoured, and

unpaid task of observation. Flamsteed and
Herschel, in their glazed observatories, may
catalogue the stars with the praise of all men,
and, the results being splendid and useful,
honour is sure. But he, in his private obser-
vatory,—cataloguing obscure and nebulous stars
of the human mind, which as yet no man has
thought of as such; watching days and months,
sometimes, for a few facts; correcting still his old
records,—must relinquish display and immediate
fame. In the long period of his preparation he
must betray often an ignorance and shiftlessness
in popular arts, incurring the disdain of the able,
who shoulder him aside. Long must he stammer
in his speech; often forego the living for the
dead. Worse yet, he must accept—how often!—
poverty and solitude. For the ease and pleasure
of treading in the old road, accepting the fashions,
the education, the religion of society, he takes
the cross of making his own, and, of course, the
self-accusation, the faint heart, the frequent un-
certainty and loss of time, which are the nettles
and tangling vines in the way of the self-relying
and self-directed; and the state of virtual hostility
in which he seems to stand to society, and
especially to educated society.

"For all this loss and scorn, what offset? He
is to find consolation in exercising the highest
functions of human nature. He is one who raises
himself from private considerations, and breathes

and lives on public and illustrious thoughts. He
is the world's eye. He is the world's heart.
He is to resist the vulgar prosperity that retro-
grades ever to barbarism, by preserving and com-
municating heroic sentiments, noble biographies,
melodious verse, and the conclusions of history.
Whatsoever oracles the human heart in all emer-
gencies, in all solemn hours, has uttered as its
commentary on the world of action—these he
shall receive and impart. And whatsoever new
verdict Reason, from her inviolable seat, pro-
nounces on the passing men and events of to-day
—this he shall hear and promulgate. These being
his functions, it becomes him to feel all confidence
in himself, and to defer never to the popular cry.
He, and he only, knows the world. The world of
any moment is the merest appearance. Some
great decorum, some fetish of a government, some
ephemeral trade, or war, or man, is cried up by
half mankind, and cried down by the other half,
as if all depended on this particular up or down.
The odds are that the whole question is not worth
the poorest thought which the scholar has lost
in listening to the controversy. Let him not quit
his belief that a popgun is a popgun, though the
ancient and honourable of the earth affirm it to
be the crack of doom. In silence, in steadiness,
in severe abstraction, let him hold by himself;
add observation to observation, patient of neglect,
patient of reproach ; and bide his own time,—

happy enough, if he can satisfy himself alone, that this day he has done something truly. Success treads on every right step. For the instinct is sure that prompts him to tell his brother what he thinks.

" He then learns that in going down into the secrets of his own mind he has descended into the secrets of all minds. He learns that he who has mastered any law in his private thoughts is master to that extent of all men whose language he speaks, and of all into whose language his own can be translated. The poet, in utter solitude remembering his spontaneous thoughts and recording them, is found to have recorded that which men ' in cities vast ' find true for them also. The orator distrusts at first the fitness of his frank confessions,—his want of knowledge of the persons he addresses,—until he finds that he is the complement of his hearers ; that they drink his words because he fulfils for them their own nature ; the deeper he dives into his privatest, secretest presentiment, to his wonder he finds, this is the most acceptable, most public, and universally true. The people delight in it ; the better part of every man feels : This is my music ; this is myself.

" For this self-trust, the reason is deeper than can be fathomed—darker than can be enlightened.

" I might not carry with me the feeling of my audience in stating my own belief. But I have

already shown the ground of my hope in ad-
verting to the doctrine that man is one. I
believe man has been wronged; he has wronged
himself. He has almost lost the light that can
lead him back to his prerogatives. Men are
become of no account. Men in history, men in
the world of to-day, are beetles, are spawn, and
are called 'the mass,' and 'the herd.' [Novalis:
Man is the temple of the living God.]

"In a century, in a millennium, one or two men;
that is to say, one or two approximations to the
right state of every man. All the rest behold in
the hero or the poet their own green and crude
being,—ripened; yes, and are content to be less,
so that he may attain to his full stature. What
a testimony—full of grandeur, full of pity—is
borne to the demands of his own nature, by the
poor clansman, the poor partisan, who rejoices in
the glory of his chief! The poor and low find
some amends, in their immense moral capacity,
for their acquiescence in a political and social
inferiority. They are content to be brushed like
flies from the path of a great person, so that
justice shall be done by him to that common
nature which it is the dearest desire of all to see
enlarged and glorified. They sun themselves in
the great man's light, and feel it to be their own
element. They cast the dignity of man from
their downtrod selves upon the shoulders of a
hero, and will perish to add one drop of blood to

make that great heart beat, those giant sinews combat and conquer. He lives for us, and we live for him."

I will now, before concluding, quote some of Emerson's poems.

The first one shall be the intensely patriotic "Boston Hymn," read by Emerson himself in the Music Hall, on January 1st, 1863.

BOSTON HYMN.

The word of the Lord by night
To the watching Pilgrims came,
As they sat by the seaside,
And filled their hearts with flame.

God said, I am tired of kings,
I suffer them no more ;
Up to my ear the morning brings
The outrage of the poor.

Think ye I made this ball
A field of havoc and war,
Where tyrants great and tyrants small
Might harry the weak and poor ?

My angel, his name is Freedom,—
Choose him to be your king ;
He shall cut pathways east and west,
And 'fend you with his wing.

Lo ! I uncover the land
Which I hid of old time in the west,
As the sculptor uncovers the statue
When he has wrought his best ;

7

I show Columbia, of the rocks
    Which dip their foot in the seas,
And soar to the air-born flocks
    Of clouds, and the boreal fleece.

I will divide my goods ;
    Call in the wretch and slave ;
None shall rule but the humble,
    And none but Toil shall have.

I will have never a noble,
    No lineage counted great ;
Fishers and choppers and ploughmen
    Shall constitute a state.

Go, cut down trees in the forest,
    And trim the straightest boughs ;
Cut down the trees in the forest,
    And build me a wooden house.

Call the people together,
    The young men and the sires,
The digger in the harvest field,
    Hireling, and him that hires ;

And here in a pine state-house
    They shall choose men to rule
In every needful faculty,
    In church, and state, and school.

Lo, now ! if these poor men
    Can govern the land and sea,
And make just laws below the sun,
    As planets faithful be.

And ye shall succour men :
    'Tis nobleness to serve ;
Help them who cannot help again ;
    Beware from right to swerve.

I break **your** bonds and masterships,
    And I unchain the slave ;
Free be his heart and hand henceforth
    As wind and wandering wave.

I cause from every creature
    His proper good to flow :
As much as he is and **doeth**,
    So much he shall **bestow**.

But laying hands on another
    To coin his labour and sweat,
He goes in pawn to his victim
    For eternal years in debt.

To-day unbind the captive—
    So only are ye unbound ;
Lift up a people from the dust,
    Trumpet of rescue sound !

Pay ransom to the owner,
    And fill the bag to the brim.
Who is the owner ?   The slave is owner,
    And ever was.   Pay him.

O North ! give him beauty for rags,
    And honour, O South ! for his shame.
Nevada ! coin thy golden crags
    With Freedom's image and name.

Up ! and the dusky **race**
    That sat in darkness long,
Be swift their **feet** as antelopes,
    And as Behemoth strong.

Come, East and **West and North**,
    By races, as snowflakes,
And carry my purpose forth,
    Which neither halts nor shakes.

My will fulfilled shall be,
For, in daylight or in dark,
My thunderbolt has eyes to see
His way home to the mark.

I will now quote an exquisitely lovely and suggestive poem on

BEAUTY.

Was never form and never face
So sweet to Seyd as only grace,

Which did not slumber like a stone,
But hover'd gleaming and was gone.

Beauty chased he everywhere,
In flame, in storm, in clouds of air.

He smote the lake to feed his eye
With the beryl beam of the broken wave ;

He flung in pebbles well to hear
The moment's music which they gave.

Oft peal'd for him a lofty tone
From nodding pole and belting zone.

He heard a voice none else could hear
From central and from errant sphere.

The quaking earth did quake in rhyme,
Seas ebbed and flowed in epic chime.

In dens of passion, and pits of woe,
He saw strong Eros struggling through,

To sun the dark and solve the curse,
And beam to the bounds of the universe.

While thus to love he gave his days
In loyal worship, scorning praise,

How spread their lures for him in vain
Thieving Ambition and paltering Gain !

He thought it happier to be dead,
To die for beauty than live for bread.

The last poem I shall ask your deep admiration
for is

NEMESIS.

Already blushes in thy cheek
The bosom-thought which thou must speak ;
The bird, how far it haply roam
By cloud or isle, is flying home ;
The maiden fears, and fearing runs
Into the charmèd snare she shuns ;
And every man, in love or pride,
Of his fate is never wide.

Will a woman's fan the ocean smooth ?
Or prayers the stony Parcæ soothe,
Or coax the thunder from its mark ?
Or tapers light the Chaos dark ?
In spite of Virtue and the Muse,
Nemesis will have her dues,
And all our struggles and our toils
Tighter wind the giant coils.

Now, I will not add any weak words of mine to
the exquisite music of Emerson's muse.

If I have said anything that will induce any
of my readers to study him more thoroughly, I

shall be quite satisfied with the result of my little sketch.

The eye sees what it brings the capacity to see. That is especially true of the mind's eye. Therefore the more we study, think, and feel, the better able we shall be to comprehend and love the spiritual and heaven-scaling genius of the American Plato.

IV.

ROBERT BROWNING.

ROBERT BROWNING was born at Camberwell on May 7th, 1812, and died at Venice on December 13th, 1889. His father was, like so many others, a writer of a great deal of unpublished verse of rather an old-fashioned didactic character. Robert began to write poetry at a very early age, and was also fond of drawing. He did not become a painter ; but, as we all know, developed into one of the greatest poets and subtlest and strongest thinkers of the century. He ardently studied the works of Keats, Shelley, Scott, Byron, Wordsworth, and Coleridge. We all know how intensely he admired and loved the glorious Shelley. Fortunately his father withheld his youthful effusions from the public ; but in after years some of the manuscripts fell into the great poet's hands, and he discovered that he had been an ardent admirer and imitator of Byron, and that his verse was "full and melodious." From the worship of Byron the boy naturally soared to a love of Shelley directly he accidentally became possessor of a piratical copy of his exquisite poems. Even

three years after Shelley's death it was very
difficult to obtain a copy of his works. No
respectable bookseller would even acknowledge
that he was acquainted with his name. Mrs.
Browning at last obtained from Messrs. Ollier,
the publishers, the original editions of both
Shelley and Keats, and presented them to her
son. Let us pause for a moment and try, in some
degree, to imagine the rapture of delight ex-
perienced by the boy-poet as he turned the leaves
containing the poems of these glorious master
singers ! But, although he loved and admired
them both so profoundly, he never imitated either.
In 1826 young Browning went to school at
Dulwich, and later to University College, London.
Six years after, in 1832, he wrote " Pauline," and
published it in 1833, when twenty-one. The
poem is dated Richmond, October 22nd, 1832. In
the same year Tennyson published " The Miller's
Daughter," "The Dream of Fair Women," " The
Palace of Art," and other of his most beautiful
and popular poems. " Pauline " was almost un-
noticed ; but it was so greatly admired by Dante
Gabriel Rossetti, then a very young man, that
he copied the whole of the poem from the book
in the British Museum. John Stuart Mill, too,
desired to review it in *Tait's Magazine;* but it
had already been dismissed by that periodical
with contempt. Fortunately the poet was not
dependent for fame and fortune or vulgar bread

and cheese upon the wisdom and critical powers
of the editor of that luminous periodical or of any
other ! If he had been, the result would have
been starvation.   Genius is certain to conquer in
the end ; but in the meantime the poet is face to
face with famine.   We must admit that out of
one hundred volumes of verse published, ninety-
nine are very likely to be bad or indifferent ; but
the man of real critical power and insight should
be on the look out for the exception, and should,
in addition, feel a pleasure in introducing it to
a public eager to welcome originality and real
power—"there are so many echoes and so few
voices."

In 1834 Mr. Browning set out on his travels,
which extended to Russia.   A year before he wrote
" Porphyria's Lover " and " Joannes Agricola."
These and other short poems were printed in
a Unitarian magazine, *The Monthly Repository*,
edited by Mr. W. Johnson Fox, afterwards member of Parliament for Oldham.   " Paracelsus "
was published in 1835.   In this poem Browning
showed his daring originality, his utter disregard
and apparent contempt for the conventional forms
of fashionable poetry ; and in the long soliloquies
he displayed the germ of that profound insight
into the workings of the heart and conscience so
wonderfully manifested in his " Bishop Blougram,"
" Andrea del Sarto," and other masterpieces in
" Men and Women."   Macready's admiration for

this poem, "Paracelsus," led to the meeting of the
great poet and actor. The latter hoped he had
found a real dramatic genius ; and those hopes
led to the production on the stage of *Strafford*,
which took place on May 1st, 1837, the poet then
being only twenty-five. Miss Helen Faucit per-
formed with grace and charm the part of Lady
Carlisle ; Macready sustained the character of
Strafford. The play was withdrawn after the
fifth night ; it was not a financial success. But
what a splendid masterpiece for a young man of
twenty-five to write ! The wonder to me is not
that it did not run over five nights, but that such
a play, so full of genius, poetry, and exalted
thought and passion, should see the footlights
at all ! Let us again thank Heaven that Browning
was independent, and that he could, in spite of
every possible discouragement and disappointment, pursue the course marked out by his splendid
genius, without heeding the cackle of blame or
the sneers of envy and mediocrity ! He wrote more
plays, which managers and publishers returned
with and without thanks. In 1840 he published his
most daringly enigmatic poem, "Sordello," as if
in defiance of his critics ; and we must admit that
even his most enthusiastic admirers have been
conquered by the inextricable jungle of thought
contained in this unique poem. Between 1841
and 1846 he published, in pamphlet form, "Bells
and Pomegranates." These were issued cheaply

for, as the author said, " a pit audience " ; but,
unfortunately, the pit audience did not arise from
that deep place to welcome them. The first of
the series was that lovely and powerful and tragic
dramatic poem, " Pippa Passes," which alone
marks with triumphant certainty Robert Browning
as a poet for all time. This was followed by
" King Viator and King Charles," and that masterpiece of marvellous word-painting, wit, humour,
and poetry, " The Pied Piper," originally written
to please Macready's son. Lucky boy ! The
rest of the series are nearly all included in " Men
and Women." However people may differ about
the merits or demerits of " Paracelsus " and "Sordello," no one, with the slenderest pretension to
a love of literature in its highest form, can
possibly differ about the beauty, the variety, the
insight into the heart and conscience of many-
sided, suffering, hoping, and struggling humanity,
displayed in this splendid work of a man of
genius whose name will live as long as a love of
English literature exists in our minds and hearts.

While Mr. Browning was writing " Bells and
Pomegranates," he was dragged down into the
miserable intrigues and petty jealousies which
beset the stage. There were quarrels with Macready, who was notoriously a man of overbearing
temper, and who seems in his relations with the
poet to have lacked candour and directness. *The
Blot in the Scutcheon* was produced, and the

play drew fairly well until Macready closed his theatre.

In 1846, September 12th, Mr. Browning married the already famous poet, Elizabeth Barrett. They started for Italy, which became their home for many years.

In September 1855 the poet dedicated " Men and Women " to his wife, in the following exquisite lines :—

> " This to you—yourself, my moon of poets !
>   Ah ! but that's the world's side, there's the wonder ;
>   Thus they see you, praise you, think they know you !
>   There, in turn, I stand with them and praise you.
>   Out of my own self, I dare to phrase it.
>   But the best is when I glide from out them,
>   Cross a step or two of dubious twilight,
>   Come out on the other side, the novel
>   Silent silver lights and darks undreamed of,
>   When I hush and bless myself with silence."

Italy continued to be Mr. Browning's home until the death of his beloved wife, which terrible loss occurred in 1861. The poet published in 1871 " Balaustion's Adventure," a transcript from Euripides, which is one of the most delightful productions of his genius. This was preceded by " Dramatis Personæ," which contains some of his noblest work, "Abt Vogler" being especially beautiful and sublime ; and his longest dramatic poem, " The Ring and the Book," which is as full of marvellous mastery of knowledge and detail as the best work of Carlyle. His great analytical power and imaginative insight into character are triumphantly displayed in this most characteristic work of the great poet.

As proved by his poems "Christmas Eve" and "Easter Day," Mr Browning was a man of deep religious conviction. He was a Nonconformist, and for many years he attended the sermons of the Rev. Thomas Jones, at the Congregational Chapel, Charrington Street, Oakley Square. After the death of Mr. Jones, the poet wrote a preface to his published sermons.

The following letter was written by Browning in 1876 to a lady, who, believing herself to be dying, wrote to thank him for the help she had derived from his poems, mentioning particularly "Rabbi ben Ezra" and "Abt Vogler."

"19, WARWICK CRESCENT, W.,
"*May* 11*th*, '76.

"DEAR FRIEND,—It would ill become me to waste a word on my own feelings, except inasmuch as they can be common to us both in such a situation as you describe yours to be—and which, by sympathy, I can make mine by the anticipation of a few years at most. It is a great thing—the greatest—that a human being should have passed the probation of life, and sum up its experience in a witness to the power and love of God. I dare congratulate you. All the help I can offer, in my poor degree, is the assurance that I see ever more

reason to hold by the same hope—and that by no
means in ignorance of what has been advanced to
the contrary ; and for your sake I would wish it
to be true that I had so much of ' genius ' as to
permit the testimony of an especially privileged
insight to come in aid of the ordinary argument.
For I know I myself have been aware of the
communication of something more subtle than
a ratiocinative process, when the convictions of
' genius ' have thrilled my soul to its depths, as
when Napoleon, shutting up the New Testament,
said of Christ : ' Do you know that I am an
understander of men ?   Well, He was no man ! '
(' *Savez-vous que je me connais en hommes ?   Eh
bien, Celui-là ne fut pas un homme.*') Or as
when Charles Lamb, in a gay fancy with some
friends as to how he and they would feel if the
greatest of the dead were to appear suddenly in
flesh and blood once more—on the final suggestion, ' And if Christ entered this room ? ' changed
his manner at once, and stuttered out—as his
manner was when moved, ' You see—if Shakespeare entered, we should all rise; if *He* appeared,
we must kneel.'   Or, not to multiply instances,
as when Dante wrote what I will transcribe from
my wife's Testament—wherein I recorded it
fourteen years ago, ' Thus I believe, thus I affirm,
thus I am certain it is, that from this life I shall
pass to another better, there, where that Lady
lives, of whom my soul was enamoured.'   Dear

Friend, I may have wearied you in spite of your good will. God bless you, sustain, and receive you! Reciprocate this blessing with

      "Yours affectionately,

           "ROBERT BROWNING."

In private life Mr. Browning was cordial and sympathetic, his conversation being full of intelligence, naturalness, and humour. He was passionately fond of music, and his fine head and noble leonine countenance were often to be seen at the Monday Popular Concerts.

"Asolando : Fancies and Facts" was published a few days before the death of the author. He lived long enough to hear of its success.

Listen to the following lines written by a poet of seventy-seven, yet full of the brightest wit and sweetest melody :—

> "Ah! the bird-like fluting
>   Through the ash-tops yonder—
> Bullfinch-bubblings, soft sounds suiting
>   What sweet thoughts, I wonder ?
> Fine-pearled notes that surely
>   Gather, dewdrop-fashion,
> Deep-down in some heart which purely
>   Secretes globuled passion—
> Passion insuppressive—
>   Such is piped, for certain ;
> Love, no doubt, nay, love excessive
>   'Tis, your ash-tops curtain."

In the unconquerable spirit of faith, youth, and

love, Robert Browning reminds me of Victor
Hugo ; and also for his Titanic strength and
exquisite tenderness.

The following lines from the last gift of the
poet to the world are full of the rarest insight
and delicacy :—

> " What girl but, having gathered flowers,
> Stript the beds and spoilt the bowers,
> From the lapful light she carries
> Drops a careless bud ?—nor tarries
> To regain the waif and stray :
> ' Store enough for home '—she'll say.

> " So say I too : give your lover
> Heaps of loving—under, over,
> Whelm him—make the one the wealthy !
> Am I all so poor who—stealthy
> Work it was !—picked up what fell :
> Not the worst bud—who can tell ? "

My object will be to present what I consider
the best of Robert Browning's work in all its
splendid variety and glorious, many-sided beauty.

But before quoting further from the great
poet, I think it would be interesting to cite
Mr. Russell Lowell's—who has many points of
genius in which he resembles Robert Browning—
speech on the poet made at a meeting of the
Browning Society.

Mr. Lowell, before concluding, said—

" The fashion of this world passed away, but
the fashion of those things which belonged to

the world of imagination—and it was most em-
phatically in that world that Mr. Browning had
worked—endured and never passed.   In 1848
Mr. Browning said, in a preface to a collection of
his poems, that many of them were out of print,
and of the rest a great number had been withdrawn from circulation—which implied that even
at that time the size of his public was very small.
But he had fully demonstrated that he stood in
no need of a Browning Society to reinforce his
native vigour; for, in spite of the indifference of
the public, he had constantly gone on from that
time to this producing and deepening the impression which he had made upon all thinking minds.
It had been said that he had no sense of form,
but that question depended on the meaning to be
attached to the word.   One thing he thought
was certain, and that was that men who had
discussed form most, as for instance Goethe, had
not always been the most successful in producing
examples of it.   Certainly no one with any sense
of form could call *Faust* other than formless.   If
form meant the use of adequate and harmonious
means to produce a certain artistic end, then he
knew no one who had given truer examples of it
than the great poet after whom that Society took
its name. . . . Every one who read Browning with
attention, and who loved him, must at the same
time admit that he was occasionally whirled away
by the sweep and torrent of his abundance.   But

after making these deductions, there was no poet
who had given us a greater variety, or who had
shown more originality. Mr. Browning abode
with them. He was not a fashion, nor did he
belong to any one period of their lives. What
they felt more clearly than anything else was
his strength. He was of all others a masculine,
a virile poet."

I would submit to you my opinion that Browning's sweetness was equal to his strength, and
his intellectual subtlety and extraordinary dia-
lectical power greater than either ; and as for
his humour, I think it almost Shakespearian in
its sunny glow and genial breadth of toleration
and sympathy with every possibility of human
nature.

The rest of this paper will be devoted to an
attempt to prove to the reader the truth of this
opinion.

PROSPICE.

Fear death ?—to feel the fog in my throat,
    The mist in my face,
When the snows begin, and the blasts denote
    I am nearing the place,
The power of the night, the press of the storm,
    The post of the foe :
Where he stands, the Arch Fear in a visible form,
    Yet the strongest man must go :
For the journey is done and the summit attained,
    And the barriers fall,
Though a battle's to fight e'er the guerdon be
        gained,
    The reward of it all.
I was ever a fighter, so—one fight more,
    The best and the last !

I would hate that death bandaged my eyes, and
        forebore,
    And bade me creep past.
No ! let me taste the whole of it, fare like my
        peers,
    The heroes of old,
Bear the brunt, in a minute pay glad life's
        arrears
    Of pain, darkness, and cold.
For sudden the worst turns the best to the brave,
    The black minute's at end,
And the elements' rage, the fiend voices that rave,
    Shall dwindle, shall blend,

Shall change, shall become first a peace out of
        pain,
    Then a joy, then a light, then thy breast,
O thou soul of my soul! I shall clasp thee
        again,
    And with God be the rest!

That glorious, soul-inspiring poem is beyond
the reach of praise : it shines like a fixed star.

The following is from

RABBI BEN EZRA.

Not on the vulgar mass
Called " work " shall sentence pass—
Things done, that took the eye and had the price,
 O'er which, from level stand,
 The low world laid its hand,
Found straightway to its mind, could value in a
  trice :
 But all, the world's coarse thumb
 And finger could not plumb,
So passed in making up the main account :
 Though hardly to be packed
 Into a narrow act,
Fancies that broke through language and escaped;
 All I could never be,
 All, men ignored in me,
This, I was worth to God, whose wheel the
  pitcher shaped.
 Ay, note the Potter's wheel,
 That metaphor ! and feel
Why time spins fast, why passive lies our clay,—
 Thou, to whom fools propound,
 When the wine makes its round,
" Since life fleets, all is change ; the past gone,
  seize to-day ! "
 Fool ! All that is, at all,
 Lasts ever, past recall ;

Earth changes, but thy soul and God stand sure:
　　　What entered into thee,
　　　That was, is, and shall be :
Time's wheel runs back or stops ; Potter and
　　　clay endure.

　　　He fixed thee mid this dance
　　　Of plastic circumstance,
This present, thou, forsooth, wouldst fain arrest :
　　　Machinery just meant
　　　To give the soul its bent,
Try thee and turn thee forth, sufficiently im-
　　　pressed.

　　　What though the earlier grooves
　　　Which ran the laughing loves
Around thy base, no longer pause and press ?
　　　What though, about thy rim
　　　Skull things, in order grim,
Grow out, in graver mood, obey the sterner
　　　stress ?
　　　Look not thou down, but up !
　　　To uses of a cup,
The festal board, lamp's flash and trumpet's peal,
　　　The new wine's foaming flow,
　　　The Master's lips aglow !
Thou, heaven's consummate cup, what wouldst thou
　　　with earth's wheel ?

ABT VOGLER.

*(After he has been extemporising upon the musical
instrument of his invention.)*

Would that the structure brave, the manifold
  music I build,
 Bidding my organ obey, calling its keys to the
  work,
Claiming each slave of the sound, at a touch, as
  when Solomon willed
 Armies of angels that soar, legions of demons
  that lurk,
Man, brute, reptile, fly, alien of end and of
  aim,
 Adverse each from the other, heaven-high,
  hell-deep removed,
Should rush into sight at once as he named the
  ineffable Name,
 And pile him a palace straight, to pleasure the
  princess he loved.

Would it might tarry like his, the beautiful
  building of mine,
 This which my keys in a crowd pressed and
  importuned to raise !
Ah ! one and all, how they helped, would dispart
  now and now combine,
 Zealous to hasten the work, heighten their
  master his praise !

And one would bury his brow with a blind plunge
    down to hell,
    Burrow awhile and build, broad on the roots of
        things,
Then up again swim into sight, having based me
    my palace well,
    Founded it, fearless of flame, flat on the nether
        springs.

And another would mount and march, like the
    excellent minion he was,
    Ay, another and yet another, one crowd but
        with many a crest,
Raising my rampired walls of gold as transparent
    as glass,
    Eager to do and die, yield each his place to the
        rest :
For higher still and higher (as a runner tips with
    fire,
    When a great illumination surprises a festal
        night—
Outlining round and round Rome's dome from
    space to spire),
    Up, the pinnacled glory reached, and the pride
    of my soul was in sight.

In sight ? Not half ! for it seemed, it was certain
    to match man's birth,
    Nature in turn conceived, obeying an impulse
    as I ;

And the emulous heaven yearned down, made
    effort to reach the earth,
  As the earth had done her best, in my passion,
    to reach the sky:
Novel splendours burst forth, grew familiar and
    dwelt with mine,
  Not a point or peak but found and fixed its
    wandering star;
Meteor moons, balls of blaze; and they did not
    pale nor pine,
  For earth had attained to heaven, there was
    no more near nor far.

Nay, more; for there wanted not, who walked in
    the glare and glow,
  Presences plain in the place; or, fresh from
    the Protoplast,
Furnished for ages to come, when a kindlier wind
    should blow,
  Lured now to begin and live, in a house to
    their liking at last;
Or else the wonderful Dead, who have passed
    through the body and gone,
  But were back once more to breathe in an old
    world worth their new:
What never had been, was now; what was, as it
    shall be soon;
  And what is,—shall I say matched both? for
    I was made perfect too.

All through my keys that gave their sounds to a
    wish of my soul,
    All through my soul that praised as its wish
        flowed visibly forth,
All through music and me !   For think, had I
    painted the whole,
    Why, there it had stood, to see, nor the pro-
        cess so wonder worth :
Had I written the same, made verse—still, effect
    proceeds from cause,
    Ye know why the forms are fair, ye hear how
        the tale is told ;
It is all triumphant art, but art in obedience
    to laws,
    Painter and poet are proud in the artist list
        enrolled ;—

But here is the finger of God, a flash of the will
    that can,
    Existent behind all laws, that made them—
        and, lo, they are !
And I know not if, save in this, such a gift be
    allowed to man,
    That out of three sounds he frame, not a fourth
        sound, but a star.
Consider it well : each tone of the scale in itself
    is nought ;
    It is everywhere in the world—loud, soft, and
        all is said :

Give it to me to use ! I mix it with two in my
    thought ;
  And, there ! Ye have heard and seen : con-
    sider and bow the head !
Well, it is gone at last, the palace of music I
    reared !
  Gone ! and the good tears start, the praises
    that come too slow ;
For one is assured at first, one scarce can say
    that he feared,
  That he even gave it a thought, the gone thing
    was to go.
Never to be again ! But many more of the
    kind
  As good, nay, better perchance. Is this your
    comfort to me,—
To me, who must be saved because I cling with
    my mind
  To the same, same self, same love, same God ?
    Ay, what was, shall be.

Therefore, to whom turn I, but to Thee, the
    ineffable Name ?
  Builder and Maker, Thou, of houses not made
    with hands !
What, have fear of change from Thee who art
    ever the same ?
  Doubt that Thy power can fill the heart that
    Thy power expands ?

There shall never be one lost good ! What was,
　　shall live as before.
　The evil is null, is nought, is silence implying
　　sound ;
What was good, shall be good, with, for evil, so
　　much good more ;
　On the earth the broken arcs ; in the heaven,
　　the perfect round.

All we have willed or hoped or dreamed of good
　　shall exist ;
　Not its semblance, but itself ; no beauty, nor
　　good, nor power,
Whose voice has gone forth, but each survives
　　for the melodist,
　When eternity affirms the conception of an
　　hour.
The high that proved too high, the heroic for
　　earth too hard,
　The passion that left the ground to lose itself
　　in the sky,
Are music sent up to God by the lover and the
　　bard ;
　Enough that he heard it once ; we shall hear
　　it by-and-by.

And what is our failure here but a triumph's
　　evidence
　For the fulness of the days ? Have we
　　withered or agonized ?

Why else was the pause prolonged, but that
    singing might issue thence ?
  Why rushed the discords in, but that harmony
    should be prized ?
Sorrow is hard to bear, and doubt is slow to
    clear,
  Each sufferer says his say, his scheme of the
    weal and woe :
But God has a few of us whom He whispers in
    the ear ;
  The rest may reason and welcome : 'tis we
    musicians know.

If the Shakespeare of music, Beethoven, had
written a poem, it would have been similar to
" Abt Vogler."

Now to show the lighter and humorous, with a subtle touch of sadness, side of Browning's genius.

YOUTH AND ART.

It once might have been—once only :
We lodged in a street together :
   You a sparrow on the housetop lonely,
I, a lone she-bird of his feather.

   Your trade was with sticks and clay,
You thumbed, thrust, patted, and polished,
   Then laughed, "They will see some day
Smith made, and Gibson demolished."

   My business was song, song, song ;
I chirped, cheeped, trilled, and twittered,
   "Kate Brown's on the boards ere long
And Grisi's existence embittered !"

   I earned no more by a warble
Than you by a sketch in plaster ;
   You wanted a piece of marble,
I needed a music master.

   We studied hard in our styles,
Chipped each at a crust like Hindoos ;
   For air, looked out on the tiles ;
For fun, watched each other's windows.

You lounged, like a boy of the South,
Cap and blouse—nay, a bit of a beard too ;
  Or you got it, rubbing your mouth
With fingers the clay adhered to.

  And I soon managed to find
Weak points in the flower-fence facing,
  Was forced to put up a blind,
And be safe in my corset-lacing.

  No harm !   It was not my fault
If you never turned your eyes' tail up,
  As I shook upon E *in alt.*,
Or ran the chromatic scale up :

  For spring bade the sparrows pair,
And the boys and girls gave guesses,
  And stalls in our street looked rare
With bulrush and watercresses.

  Why did not you pinch a flower
In a pellet of clay and fling it ?
  Why did not I put a power
Of thanks in a look, or sing it ?

  I did look, sharp as a lynx
(And yet the memory rankles),
  When models arrived, some minx
Tripped upstairs, she and her ankles.

  But I think I gave you as good !
" That foreign fellow,—who can know
  How she pays, in a playful mood,
For his tuning her that piano ? "

Could you say so, and never say,
" Suppose we join hands and fortunes,
  And I fetch her from over the way,
Her, piano, and long tunes and short tunes ? "

No, no, you would not be rash,
Nor I rasher and something over.
  You've to settle your Gibson's hash,
And Grisi yet lives in clover.

But you met the prince at the Board,
I'm queen myself at *bals-paré*,
  I've married a rich old lord,
And you're dubbed Knight and an R.A.

Each life unfulfilled, you see ;
It hangs still, patchy and scrappy :
  We have not sighed deep, laughed free,
Starved, feasted, despaired,—been happy.

And nobody calls you a dunce,
And people suppose me clever :
  This could but have happened once,
And we missed it, lost it for ever.

That little poem is a masterpiece of wit,
humour, and pathos.

The following poem is sublime in its scorn of vulgar popularity and cheap success :—

THE LOST LEADER.

Just for a handful of silver he left us,
 Just for a riband to stick in his coat—
Found the one gift of which fortune bereft us,
 Lost all the others she lets us devote.
They, with the gold to give, doled him out
  silver,
 So much was theirs who so little allowed :
How all our copper had gone for his service !
 Rags—were they purple, his heart had been
  proud !

We that had loved him so, followed him, honoured
  him,
 Lived in his mild and magnificent eye,
Learned his great language, caught his clear
  accents,
 Made him our pattern to live and to die !
Shakespeare was of us, Milton was for us,
 Burns, Shelley, were with us,—they watch
  from their graves !
He alone breaks from the van and the freemen,
 He alone sinks to the rear and the slaves !

We shall march prospering,—not through his
  presence ;
 Songs may inspirit us,—not from his lyre ;

Deeds will be done,—while he boasts his quies-
cence,
  Still bidding crouch whom the rest bade
  aspire :

Blot out his name, then, record one lost soul
more,
  One task more declined, one more footpath
  untrod,
One more devil's-triumph and sorrow for angels,
  One more wrong to man, one more insult to
  God !

Life's night begins : let him never come back
to us !
  There would be doubt, hesitation, and pain,
Forced praise on our part—the glimmer of
twilight,
  Never glad confident morning again !

But fight on well, for we taught him—strike
gallantly,
  Menace our heart ere we master his own ;
Then let him receive the new knowledge and
wait us,
  Pardoned in heaven, the first by the throne !

The next poem, "Evelyn Hope," is full of the poet's most subtle suggestion and exquisite charm.

EVELYN HOPE.

Beautiful Evelyn Hope is dead !
　Sit and watch by her side an hour.
That is her bookshelf, this her bed ;
　She plucked that piece of geranium-flower,
Beginning to die, too, in the glass.
　Little has yet been changed, I think :
The shutters are shut, no light may pass
　Save two long rays through the hinge's
　　chink.

Sixteen years old when she died !
　Perhaps she had scarcely heard my name ;
It was not her time to love ; beside,
　Her life had many a hope and aim,
Duties enough and little cares,
　And now was quiet, now astir,
Till God's hand beckoned unawares,
　And the sweet white brow is all of her.

Is it too late then, Evelyn Hope ?
　What, your soul was pure and true,
The good stars met in your horoscope,
　Made you of spirit, fire, and dew—

And, just because I was thrice as old,
   And our paths in the world diverged so
      wide,
Each was nought to each, must I be told?
   We were fellow-mortals, nought beside?

No, indeed! for God above
   Is great to grant, as mighty to make,
And creates the love to reward the love:
   I claim you still, for my own love's sake!
Delayed it may be for more lives yet,
   Through worlds I shall traverse, not a few:
Much is to learn and much to forget
   Ere the time be come for taking you.

But the time will come,—at last it will,
   When, Evelyn Hope, what mean (I shall
      say)
In the lower earth, in the years long still,
   That body and soul so pure and gay?
Why your hair was amber I shall divine,
   And your mouth of your own geranium's
      red—
And what you would do with me, in fine,
   In the new life come in the old one's stead.

I have lived (I shall say) so much since then,
   Given up myself so many times,
Gained me the gains of various men,
   Ransacked the ages, spoiled the climes;

Yet one thing, one, in my soul's full scope,
    Either I missed or itself missed me :
And I want and find you, Evelyn Hope !
    What is the issue ?   Let us see !

I loved you, Evelyn, all the while !
    My heart seemed full as it could hold—
There was place and to spare for the frank young
        smile
    And the red young mouth, and the hair's young
        gold.
So, hush,—I will give you this leaf to keep :
    See, I shut it inside the sweet cold hand !
There, that is our secret : go to sleep !
    You will wake, and remember, and understand.

The following little poem shows Browning's profound knowledge of human nature. It opens the very core of a woman's heart :—

A WOMAN'S LAST WORD.

Let's contend no more, Love,
    Strive nor weep ;
All be as before, Love,
    Only sleep !

What so wild as words are ?
    I and thou
In debate, as birds are,
    Hawk on bough !

See the creature stalking
    While we speak !
Hush and hide the talking,
    Cheek on cheek !

What so false as truth is,
    False to thee ?
Where the serpent's tooth is,
    Shun the tree ;

Where the apple reddens
    Never pry—
Lest we lose our Edens,
    Eve and I.

Be a god, and hold me
  With a charm !
Be a man, and fold me
  With thine arm !

Teach me, only teach, Love !
  As I ought
I will speak thy speech, Love,
  Think thy thought—

Meet, if thou require it,
  Both demands,
Laying flesh and spirit
  In thy hands.

That shall be to-morrow,
  Not to-night.
I must bury sorrow
  Out of sight :

Must a little weep, Love
  (Foolish me !),
And so fall asleep, Love,
  Loved by thee.

MY STAR.

All that I know
Of a certain star
  Is, it can throw
(Like the angled spar)
  Now a dart of red,
Now a dart of blue ;
  Till my friends have said
They would fain see, too,
My star that dartles the red and the blue !
Then it stoops like a bird ; like a flower hangs
    furled :
  They must solace themselves with the Saturn
    above it.
What matter to me if their star is a world ?
  Mine has opened its soul to me ; therefore I
    love it.

In that exquisite gem the English Dante cele-
brates his lost Beatrice.

By the poems quoted, I think I have proved
the universality of Browning's genius ; the
breadth of humour, the tender, exquisite pathos,
the all-penetrating insight he had into the
heights and depths of human thought, aspiration,
and passion ; and, above all, the passionate love
of truth, the manly honesty and directness of
his nature, with its intense scorn for all the

tricks of the charlatan and shallow pretender. I don't think I can conclude my paper better than by quoting the lines of the great poet's wife which were so exquisitely sung at the funeral at Westminster Abbey, when England proved not inadequately, I think, her love and veneration for Robert Browning's genius and character.

" What would we give to our beloved ?
  The hero's heart to be unmoved,
    The poet's star-tuned harp to sweep,
  The patriot's voice to teach and rouse,
  The monarch's crown to light the brows ?—
    " He giveth His belovèd sleep."

" O earth, so full of dreary noises !
  O men, with wailing in your voices !
    O delvèd gold, the wailer's heap !
  O strife, O curse, that o'er it fall !
  God strikes a silence through you all,
    And "giveth His belovèd sleep."

" His dews drop mutely on the hill,
  His cloud above it saileth still,
    Though on its slopes men sow and reap.
  More softly than the dew is shed,
  Or cloud is floated overhead,
    " He giveth His belovèd sleep."

The poems from Mr. Robert Browning's works included in this sketch are printed by special arrangement with Messrs. Smith, Elder & Co.

NOTE.

THE February number of the *Argosy* contains a very interesting article on Robert Browning. The writer, Mrs. E. F. Bridell-Fox, is the daughter of the Rev. W. J. Fox, afterwards member of Parliament for Oldham, who was the first to heartily recognise the genius of Robert Browning. Mr. Fox was then editor of the *Monthly Repository*. Browning's "Pauline," his first poem, was published in 1833, and Mr. Fox gave it the most unstinted praise. Robert Browning never forgot the cordial praise and discriminating criticism his first work received from Mr. Fox. Several of his shorter poems appeared in the *Monthly Repository*. Mrs. Bridell-Fox quotes several letters from Robert Browning to her father, and from them I shall quote some passages.

In 1833 Browning wrote as follows to his friend and critic :—

"I can only offer you my simple thanks, but they are of the sort that we can only give once or twice in a life. All things considered, I think you are almost repaid if you imagine what I feel. As for the book, I hope ere long to better it."

In the same year, the poet wrote again to his friend, and from that letter I quote the following :—

"I shall never write a line without thinking of the source of my first praise, be assured. . . ."

I regret I can only quote the following sentences from another letter to Mr. Fox.

"CASA GUIDI, January 1857.

" I wish from my heart we could get closer together again, as in those old days, and what times we would have together. . . . I would, you know I would, always would, choose you out of the whole English world to judge and correct what I write myself. My wife shall read this, and let it stand, if I have told her so, these twelve years ; and certainly I have not grown intellectually one inch over the good and kind hand you extended over my head, how many years ago ! "

The great poet's own lines alone do justice to the cordial recognition so generously accorded to the first work of Robert Browning, by Mr. W. J. Fox :—

> " Stand still, true poet that you are,
>   I know you ; let me try and draw you.
> Some night you'll fail us. When afar
>   You rise, remember one man saw you,
> Knew you, and named a star."

In addition to the very interesting letter quoted, there is a most vivid face-to-face portrait of the poet, when a young man, drawn with great skill by the hand of Mrs. Bridell-Fox, whose talent in artistic portraiture is well known, on the occasion of his calling at her father's house at Bayswater :—

" I remember that I was trying to copy Retsch's design of a young knight surrounded by Undines, who seek to entice him down with them into the waves, when Mr. Browning entered the little drawing-room, with a quick, light step, and on hearing from me that my father was out—and, in fact, that nobody was at home except myself—he said : 'It's my birthday to-day ; I'll wait till they come in,' and sitting down to the piano, he added : 'If it won't disturb you, I'll play till they return.' And as he turned to the instrument, the bells of some neighbouring church suddenly burst forth with a frantic, merry peal. It seemed to my childish fancy as if in response to his remark that it was his birthday. He was then slim and dark, and very handsome ; and— may I just hint it ?—just a trifle of a dandy, addicted to lemon-coloured kid gloves, and such things, quite the glass of fashion and the mould of form ! But full of ambition, eager for success, eager for fame, and what's more, determined to conquer and achieve success."

THE END.

Printed by Hazell, Watson & Viney, Ld., London and Aylesbury.

Mr. Joseph Forster's Lectures

ON

GREAT WRITERS AND SPEAKERS

English, French, German, and Spanish.

ILLUSTRATED BY

Dramatic Readings and Recitations.

Vivid Biographical and Analytical Sketches of the following Authors :—

CARLYLE, EMERSON, RUSKIN, BROWNING, BURNS, DICKENS, THACKERAY, HOOD, SHELLEY, COLERIDGE.

German Writers.

GOETHE (4 LECTURES), SCHILLER, LESSING, RICHTER, HEINE.

French Writers.

MARIVAUX, VOLTAIRE, DIDEROT, ROUSSEAU, BEAU-MARCHAIS, BÉRANGER, MIRABEAU, DANTON AND ROBESPIERRE, VICTOR HUGO, AND MR. FORSTER'S VERSION OF COMTE ALFRED DE VIGNY'S TRAGEDY, "CHATTERTON."

Spanish Writers.

LOPE DE VEGA, CALDERON, CERVANTES.

[*For Press Notices see Following Pages.*]

A FEW PRESS NOTICES.

" *London Society* contains a lively chat on Beaumarchais, though it omits the wittiest thing that was said in connection with the famous lawsuit. Beaumarchais had been 'blâmé' by the Court, the consequences of 'blâmé' resembling those of 'civil death.' Public sympathy being with him, however, he paraded his stigma a little too ostentatiously, till an acquaintance dryly observed to him ' *Monsieur, ce n'est pas assez que d'être blâmé; il faut être modeste.*'"—*St. James' Gazette and Budget,* **August 6th, 1887.**

"Mr. Joseph Forster contributes a well-written sketch of the life of the celebrated *littérateur* Diderot, from which is taken the following extract:— 'The most tragic event in Diderot's life was the treachery of the rascally printer, who, after Diderot had corrected the proofs for the remaining volumes of the Encyclopædia, which were to be launched simultaneously, cut out all the best parts of the articles on his ignorant estimate of the danger there would be in their publication, and, to the infinite grief and mad despair of Diderot, the grand work of his life was truncated and nearly spoiled by an ignorant rascal of a printer. Still, even in its present form, the Encyclopædia exists, a monument to the industry, the genius, and the courage of the great man who conceived the idea, and worked with unflagging ardour and dauntless courage to give that idea form and substance.'"—*Manchester Guardian,* November 10th, 1886.

"Mr. Joseph Forster has a highly appreciative article on Thackeray, in which the goodness of heart of the great novelist is justly extolled."—*Morning Post,* February 2nd, 1888.

"Mr. Joseph Forster contributes a notice of 'Thackeray,' in which he is a little too contemptuous of the 'Philistines' who fail to recognise an immeasurable genius, and persist in saying they cannot shut their eyes to a strain of cynicism, in that very powerful novelist and satirist."—*Pictorial World,* February 9th, 1888.

"An article on Thackeray, by Joseph Forster, will be read with satisfaction."— *The Queen,* February 11th, 1888.

"'William Makepeace Thackeray,' by Joseph Forster, is written with sincere and loving appreciation of the distinguished satirist, and contains many illustrations of the 'nobility, beauty, and tenderness of his genius.'"—*Life,* February 2nd, 1888.

"There is a pleasant paper on Thackeray in *London Society.* The writer, Mr. Forster, defends him from the charge of being a cynic. I am always reading such defences as these, but I never met a person of any education who thought Thackeray cynical."—*England,* February 11th, 1888.

"About the best article in the number (*Time,* of November) is one by Mr. Joseph Forster on Diderot."—*Birmingham Daily Post,* November 2nd, 1886.

"A curious and significant sight was witnessed at the Limehouse Town Hall last night, when a crowded meeting, largely composed of the poorest of the labouring classes of the district, listened with appreciation and delight to a lecture by Mr.

Joseph Forster on **Victor** Hugo. **The Common** Council, we know, does **not** approve of the great Frenchman, or **care to** pay **him** the honour that it is commonly so forward to offer to moneyed or titled insignificance. But among the workmen of London, whose approbation he would certainly have valued far more, Victor Hugo is held in high esteem. The genuineness of this feeling is shown by the fact that so many of the metropolitan candidates found it worth while to be present at, or in some way associate their names with, the meeting **of** last **night. . . . The** meeting was a thorough success, and should be a reproach to those who accuse the English workman of insularity and of a soul that cannot rise above his own **material interests.** Here is an undoubted case of enthusiasm for a great man, and that **man a** foreigner, purely on **the ground** of his intellectual and moral gifts."—*Pall Mall Gazette*, July 24th, 1885.

" **An admirable sketch of Ruskin, with choice passages from his writings.**"— *Leeds Mercury*, November 3rd, 1887.

. . . "And, what will be of infinite **interest to all** readers, the first part of a series of articles on John Ruskin. Mr. **Joseph Forster, who** is responsible for these papers, illustrates the 'Master's' **character by copious** extracts from his writings. **But he** is not backward in expressing an independent opinion. This is what Mr. Forster says about him :—

" John Ruskin, with a chivalrous disregard of the wear-and-tear consequent upon mingling in the dusty daily fray, breaks out here with a letter, and there with a lecture, dealing directly with the topic of the hour. He is constantly tapped by the foolishest people. . . . To those who can weigh, measure, and discriminate between his opinions, and as a noble and chivalrous denouncer of the infinite vulgarity and stupid greed of the age, his teachings are of unspeakable value.' " —*Sheffield Daily Telegraph*, October 27th, 1887.

"**The best of** the miscellaneous articles is Mr. Joseph **Forster's account of** Ruskin's life and work."—*Morning Post*, November 2nd, 1887.

" Mr. Joseph Forster contributes an **article of** much interest **about 'John** Ruskin,' whose numerous admirers **will,** we think, not complain of **the estimate** formed of their hero."—*The Queen*, November 19th, 1887.

"**To** some doubtless the best thing in the number [*London Society*, November] will be Mr. Joseph Forster's capital account **of Mr.** Ruskin, in which we have much information as to Mr Ruskin's ways."—*Public Opinion*, November 4th, 1887.

" There **is** one paper **on** 'John Ruskin.' It is mainly composed **of** extracts, very carefully and judiciously selected, in order to bring out the light and shade of his character and genius. We **note** one curious little point. The writer (Mr. J. Forster) **devotes a page or** two to Wordsworth, because, as he says, to understand Ruskin **it is necessary to** understand Wordsworth, adding, 'Ruskin is simply **saturated with Wordsworth.'** Now, within the last few weeks a little book has **appeared with the title, 'Books that** Have Influenced Me,' and Mr. Ruskin is **one of ten men of mark who supply** autobiographic information on this point. Mr. Ruskin gives Horace, **Pindar, Dante,** Scott, Byron, Pope, Coleridge, Keats, **Burns,** Molière, etc., but **he does not, either** in his list **or** in a supplementary letter, so much as allude to Wordsworth."—*Birmingham Daily Post*, **October 20th,** 1887.

"'**John** Ruskin,' by Joseph Forster, will have many grateful readers, choice illustrations being given of the beauty, intellectual and moral, contained in Mr. Ruskin's writings."—*Cambridge Chronicle*, November 11th, 1887.

PRESS NOTICES—continued.

"MR. JOSEPH FORSTER ON 'THOMAS CARLYLE.'—On Tuesday night Mr. Joseph Forster delivered a powerful lecture on 'Thomas Carlyle : his Life, Works, and Character,' at the Clapham Assembly Rooms. Dr. Eugene Oswald, M.A., President of the Carlyle Society, presided. Mr. Forster in his lecture gave a vivid sketch of Carlyle's father, and spoke of his attending a sermon when a preacher painted the horrors of eternal punishment. Mr. Carlyle let him finish, then left his pew, and planting himself before the clergyman, said, 'Ay, ye may stump and stare till yer een start frae their sockets, but ye'll na gar me to believe such stuff as that.' 'So much,' said the lecturer, 'for the very vertebrate father of Carlyle.' Mr. Forster then painted, from Carlyle's own words, an exquisite portrait of his mother. 'My mother stands in my memory as beautiful in all that makes the excellence of woman. Pious and gentle she was, with an unwearied devotedness to her family, a loftiness of moral aim and religious conviction which gave her presence and her humble home a sort of graciousness, and, even as I see it now, dignity, and with it, too, a good deal of wit and originality of mind. No man had better opportunities than I for comprehending, were they comprehensible, the great depths of a mother's love for her children.' Mr. Forster referred to Carlyle's literary struggle, and spoke of his contributions to the *Edinburgh Encyclopædia*, and his translation of 'Wilhelm Meister,' which Lord Jeffrey, the man who said that Wordsworth would not do, condemned as 'eminently absurd, puerile, incongruous, and affected.' . . . 'Almost from beginning to end one flagrant offence against every rule of composition.' 'That,' said the lecturer, 'is the kind of absurdity men of talent produce when they sit in judgment on a man of genius.'' Mr. Forster then referred to Carlyle's 'Life of Schiller,' which he considered one of the most fascinating biographies ever written, and which Goethe himself translated into German. Mr. Forster gave some fine selections from Carlyle's works in confirmation of his opinion of his character and genius. At the conclusion of the lecture, Mr. Forster proposed a vote of thanks to Dr. Oswald for doing him the honour of presiding. This was very cordially carried. Dr. Oswald, in returning thanks for the compliment, said that two new books were coming out which would dispel the cloud of prejudice which had gathered round the genius of Carlyle; one was his early letters, and the other the letters of Goethe and Carlyle.—*South London Press*, December 11th, 1886.

"Mr. Joseph Forster's lecture on 'Emerson,' delivered at the Crystal Palace, on Friday last, proved very interesting. In speaking of Emerson's self-trust, the lecturer said :—'A man who thinks of the success of his writing, and not of his writing only, may gain a superficial success ; he may be noticed in the *Times*, and even worse papers, but he never gains, and never deserves to gain, a hold on the brains and hearts of mankind. It is not by pleasing the vulgar that a man succeeds ; it is by pleasing the wise and discriminating, who dictate to the vulgar what to admire. Genius can only be thoroughly appreciated by genius. A man can only really be judged by his peers. But still we little people may pick up some thoughts and ideas suitable to our size, and, if we are strong enough, carry them away." Mr. Forster, in the course of his lecture, introduced, with great effect, Mr. Lowell's parallel between Carlyle and Emerson, one of the wittiest, wisest, and brightest things of that most genial writer and man."—*Society*, March 22nd, 1884.

For Terms and Dates, address :—

MR. JOSEPH FORSTER,

CARE OF MESSRS. LACON & OLLIER,

168, NEW BOND STREET, LONDON, W.

www.ingramcontent.com/pod-product-compliance
Lightning Source LLC
Chambersburg PA
CBHW030903050726
47500CB00009B/1003